MARCHING ON

AF493043

RICHARD GLESSNER

MARCHING ON

78TH REGIMENT OHIO
VETERAN VOLUNTEER INFANTRY

CIVIL WAR

Copyright © 2026 Richard Glessner

All rights reserved.

No part of this book may be reproduced, stored in a retrieval system, or transmitted in any form or by any means, electronic, mechanical, photocopying, recording, or otherwise, without prior written permission from the copyright holder, except as permitted by law.

No part of this book may be used to train artificial intelligence, machine learning models, or similar technologies without the express written permission of the copyright holder.

The text of this book was written by the author without the use of generative artificial intelligence.

ISBN: 979-8-9951572-0-5

Editorial and production services by Legacy Collection Press.

Select historical images courtesy of Glessner House.

Additional historical images courtesy of the 78th Ohio Infantry Living History Association.

"At its very core, history is a collection of stories--
a fact that makes it exciting to study.
History's stories, like all good stories, have plots, settings,
and most important, characters both major and minor."

P. Michael Jones, late Director,
General John A. Logan Museum

to William Tyre,
and the staff and trustees of

GLESSNER HOUSE
Chicago, Illinois

without whose generous assistance
this story would have been impossible.

A Word of History

"Marching On" is a historical fiction based on the true-to-life service of Lieutenant William M. Laughlin in the 78th Ohio Infantry as a wagoner in America's Civil War.

Details of his death in the Battle of Atlanta are few, as his body was never recovered. Researchers at Glessner House have determined William's war momentos, now in Glessner House collections, to have been presented to William's sister, Margaret Blocksom, by his war companion Pvt. George C. Hall.

Historical also is the death of William's wife, Mary Drake, and the couple's infant daughter, also named Mary, and their surviving son, John. History also accounts for William's younger brothers, Alexander and Samuel, and his other sister, Mary Laughlin, wife of Jacob Glessner, the couple who parented William Laughlin Glessner (the soldier's namesake) of Wheeling Steel, and John Jacob Glessner of International Harvester and Glessner House.

Making their way into "Marching On" are other historical characters, who have been given fictitious properties, for example, Frances Elizabeth Quinn, Johnny Clem, Nurse Sinnott, Marshal Yetman, and, decidedly, George C. Hall.

The author traces his ancestry to Jacob B. Glessner, pioneer brother to Henry Glessner, the grandfather of the Jacob Glessner in the novel.

Chapter One

A Misty Night - September 22, 1914

Nothing but grass and weeds surround me, except for a single rising hill. The trees bordering the meadow are as thick as a forest.

Where am I?

The cold air forces the breath from my chest. The air feels wrong, too still. I shouldn't be here, and yet I feel a strange attachment to this place.

My stomach tightens: dare I look around?

I slowly turn to one side, only to make out a distinctive shape in the fog. I move closer to examine it, and freeze. It's a person. Or rather, a body. It's nearly covered by weeds, and its limbs are charred and twisted. Its bones gleam through the bits of scorched flesh still hanging on, covered in cinders of military clothing. The acrid fumes of sticky-sweet smoke seep forth, and the smell churns my stomach.

My breath catches. I take in the angle of the jaw, the way the body is slumped, leaning forward, arms extended, as though it simply has to reach for something. My throat closes. Those are my arms. It's me!

"Oh, thank goodness!" Relief washes over me when something brushes against my arm, only to be replaced by a chill prickling my skin. An opaque, shadowy figure looms behind me, hovering only a few feet away. "Who's there?"

Chills overtake me. What is that? A human? An evil specter?

The creature points to my chest, then hooks a finger downward. What does it mean? Is it giving a command? Following its gaze, I reach for my breast pocket and feel a folded paper. It's a note, ornately decorated, but old, and damp from sweat. The shadowy specter motions for me to open it.

> Dear Chilli Will,
>
> I will be faithfully waiting for you at the end of the war. No, let me rephrase that. I promise you I will be waiting for you at the very threshold of eternity, if need be.

What does this mean? "At the close of the war." What war? Who wrote this? Who promised to wait?

Was I in a war? Come on, Will. Think, think! Something happened at this place. What was the beginning of all this?

The shadowlike form extends one finger over its shoulder, pointing to the panorama around me, and in a slow, distant voice, utters one word. "Remember."

The field dissolves: the hill, even the sky, disappears into a blur of dark color. The next thing I know, I'm falling.

Chapter Two

Zanesville, Ohio - Autumn 1860

The sweet dusty smell of hay fills my lungs as I shovel manure from my sister's husband, Jacob Glessner's, horse stall. The scrape of iron against the wooden floor helps steady me as Sam's voice echoes in the chicken yard.

The night before, the streets of Zanesville had burned with torchlight as a parade of flames bobbed through the darkness. Young men in black capes and military caps marched toward City Hall. As they came near the blacksmith shop, their glows illuminating their faces, I recognized one of them as Sam. His shoulders were square, and his chin was lifted. It was clear he had already chosen a side. I tried to catch him back then but found myself too shaken up to keep up with the marching soldiers. Instead, I waited until he bent down to feed the chickens before strolling out of the barn and dropping my shovel as I plunked myself down on a bale of hay.

"Sam, I saw you last night marching through town in a torchlight parade. What were you doing?"

"Yes," Sam squints at me, pressing his lips together. "It was a demonstration of the Wide-Awakes. Boys all over the North wake up the voters to support Mr. Lincoln in his candidacy."

There's an edge of pride beneath his shaking words, and I soften my tone. "Sit down a second, Sam. I'd like to tell you something. I, too, want Mr. Lincoln to win the election, and I think it's good that you are stirring the voters. But I won't be able to help you. I'm going to enlist. Soon."

His hands still their nervous tapping on his knee as I continue, "Some states are already seceding, even Virginia, and I won't stand by while Wheeling is dragged into a slave state. One man, one vote; not one black man counted as three-fifths, if any of us live through what's coming.

"You're going to go to war?"

"There's an infantry unit forming not far from here, commanded by Zanesville's Superintendent of Schools, Mr. Leggett. I want you to keep an eye open to give my wife Mary a hand now and then, and little Johnny, too."

"That sounds exciting!" He grins widely. "I'll be eighteen real soon. When I am, I'll join up with you."

I inhale the sweet smell of hay. "Sam, that's the other part of what I want to tell you. There's a big difference between carrying a torch and shouldering a musket."

He sets down his pail with a clink. The hens squawk. "I just want to do my part. You're going to war; why not me?" He jams his thumb into his chest.

"I'm not forbidding you, Sam. I'm protecting you from rushing into a life you know nothing about, like sleeping in swamps with rattlesnakes, and killing a man in an instant before he kills you."

Sam stares ahead. A fire wagon dashes down the road behind us, bells ringing, raising dust. "For nights now, I've talked this over with Mary and Johnny. It's not a decision you make on a whim."

Sam clicks his tongue. "You know, there'd be four of you if your daughter had not died getting born. Heavy stuff."

"It is. But my conscience won't let me do otherwise. I'll do whatever I must to preserve the Union. Mary agrees that my contribution at arms, wherever it leads, is more important than family conveniences.

I meet his gaze squarely. "You and Syd are headed toward marriage. That kind of loyalty changes things. Each of us is charged with the responsibility to figure out what duty really means. You won't really know how she feels 'til you've been married for a spell. The nice part of working in the barn is that it gives you time to ponder."

"Old Jacob Glessner can do his own barn work and ponder!"

"Jacob makes his contribution through the *Zanesville Gazette*. Do you know the power of the press, Sam? And he's pushing Lincoln's platform in the state legislature, as well."

"Really? He does that?"

"He does that."

"Tell you what, William. Sydney and I have a date Saturday night. I'll talk to her about it!"

"Talk with her, Sam. Many times. Not just on Saturday night!"

"Yes," he says. "Many Saturday nights! And I won't forget the part about the swamps and rattlesnakes!"

I hold out my hand, "Go for it, bro!"

He grabs my hand, and we strain against one another in a mock arm-wrestling competition. He laughs, strong and careless, and I force myself to match it. It's easier to grin than to admit the thought that keeps gnawing at me, that this might be the last time I see my brother as a boy.

Chapter Three

November 13, 1861

The ride, of course, is strewn with bumps. The wagon's wheels lurch on the grooves of the muddy road to Camp Gilbert. Even riding the buckboard with the wagoner doesn't help. And he doesn't sufficiently distract me. Not that it matters. My head is back in the barn, wandering back to the last comment Sam made about my family. "There might have been four of you instead of three."

"Marylee." Her name would be Mary, but we'd call her "Marylee" to distinguish her from my sister and wife. She weighed at a mere four pounds, eight ounces. My Mary was ten years younger then, and would have loved to hold a warm, pink baby in her arms. But that was not to be.

The horse whinnies: he knows his duty. I'm still trying to find mine. Just that morning, I had attempted to find answers in my sister Mary's kitchen.

Without looking up from peeling apples, she had quietly said, "I know. Wanna sit?"

I'd shaken my head. "No. My head is sloshing around like a catfish in a bucket. I just..." But, with a raised eyebrow, she stopped me in my stammering.

"William, why don't you just let it out?"

And so, I did. I asked her to help me understand, not as a sister, but as a woman. How did it feel when you carried a child only to lose her?

Mary told me everything she could. About the heaviness and the wild appetites in the flutter of tiny kicks. About the terrible force of your own organs tearing at your skin. The seemingly endless blood flow and the gouging, insufferable pain. Then she lifted an apple, bit off a big chunk, and spat it onto the counter. "Then," she said, "it's gone! Just like that!"

My wagon companion exhales a gentle, "Wo-o-oh!" and the horse's hooves stop. I blink and stare at the guard post in front of us. Off in the distance, a bugle trumpets over the tents and sheds of Camp Gilbert.

I thank my driver and place a few coins in his hand. A small price to pay for the stage I'm about to enter. No matter where this perilous journey takes me, thoughts of my wife and sisters, and even the daughter we lost, will spur me on. For there is nothing more worthy of fighting for than family.

Chapter Four

Winter finds Camp Gilbert buried in feet of snow. The cold is raw and unforgiving. The icy substance is on my legs all the way up to my knees as I wade forward, but even the most bitter of winds cannot numb the loss lodged in my chest. This is not the first time I've questioned my purpose here.

"Next!" one of the officials calls. I scramble forward and take my place in line at one of the five recruitment tables as a soldier barrels through the throng.

"Got a mule slipped on the ice and injured its fetlock! Can anyone help?"

I raise a hand, "I can."

The officer at the table waves me out of line. I follow the soldier to it. The wound is ugly but clean. I apply ointment and wrap a bandage around the mule's joint as she balances patiently on three legs.

The attendant whistles as he watches me work. "Mules, they don't hardly ever want to have one leg off the ground!

You've got an untrained Jenny eating out of your hand!" I fight back a blush and turn to reply, only to be interrupted by the scowling lieutenant looming in the doorway.

"You there, what's your name?"

"Laughlin, sir."

"When you're done, go tell the recruiter you've been selected for a wagoner. If they say they don't do it that way, tell 'em Harrison says so!"

"Y-Yes, sir," I stammer. He nods and spins on his heel to walk away, and I silently thank my sister for the years of mucking Saul and her husband's barn.

Just as Harrison expected, the recruiter argued for standard procedure: sticking me in the infantry first, and only pulling me out for a wagoner when needed. Lt. Harrison, as Quartermaster Overseer of the entire division, had his way, and I was a wagoner upon enlistment.

Four days after enlistment, my company's corporal, Joseph Starrott, calls me into his quarters with a telegram.

I knock.

"Come in!"

We salute, and he slides the yellow telegram across his desk in front of me. The look on his face reminds me that our telegrams are not sealed. I brace for the worst as my gaze drifts to the sender's name. Samuel J. Laughlin.

My hands shake as I unfold it.

```
17 NOVEMBER 1861.
PVT. WILLIAM M. LAUGHLIN.
78TH OHIO V.V. INFANTRY, COMPANY C.
```

WITH DEEP REGRET, THIS IS TO INFORM YOU
THAT YOUR WIFE, MARY DRAKE LAUGHLIN,
DIED THIS MORNING OF UNKNOWN CAUSES.
AUTOPSY TO BEGIN IMMEDIATELY.

My mouth hangs open. The room tilts.

Autopsy! I yell internally. *Autopsy!* Her sweet body being treated like some casual substance in the cold hands of some coroner? I shake my head. I can't even dare to think it, I should have been there. I should have never left. My heart sinks into my stomach.

"Soldier?" Cpl. Starrott calls. "Are you all right?"

I want to run, no sprint, back to Zanesville, to Johnny. He'll be an orphan without me, and I can't have that. My gaze shifts to the corporal, searching for any sign this isn't real.

He draws a finger across his mustache and motions for me to read on. I grip the desk to stay upright.

MR AND MRS DRAKE, HER PARENTS, ARE BEING CONSOLED.

YOU CONVINCED ME NOT TO RUSH HEADLONG INTO THE ARMY.

The barn snaps into view. Hay. Chickens. Sam's voice. My finger stops at ARMY.

I read aloud, barely breathing. "GOOD THING YOU DID, BROTHER. SYDNEY AND I WILL PROVIDE A HOME FOR YOUR SON UNTIL YOU RETURN. HE IS NOTABLY CHARMING AND COOPERATIVE FOR AN EIGHT-YEAR-OLD BOY.

LOVE, SAMUEL J. LAUGHLIN."

When I look up, the corporal simply stares at me. For a moment, my feet are bolted to his floor, like a panicked horse without a rider.

Starrott folds his hands on his desk. "You may request a

leave. Take time to think. There's a man in Company C from Zanesville, George Hall. A comrade helps in hard times."

I nod numbly, and he salutes again. "Dismissed."

I amble mindlessly across the compound and into the canteen to order coffee. My eyes land on a soldier sitting alone in the corner. He certainly looks young enough to be George Hall. Almost magnetically, I drift over to him.

"William Laughlin," I speak. "I'm going on leave soon. Corporal mentioned a Zanesville boy who may take my place. George Hall. That you?"

He nods far too enthusiastically and holds out a hand. "In the flesh!" I shake it limply, frowning slightly as his eyes narrow and he gives me a onceover. "I think I know somebody from your family in Zanesville. Ever go to Trinity Church? When I was just a kid, I had a Sunday School teacher named Miss Laughlin."

"That would be my sister, Margaret," I speak. "Her married name's Blocksom."

He nods. I join him with my coffee mug, remembering how the corporal said a comrade is a good thing to have in tough times. I soon detect, however, that George is not much help. Before it cools off enough to drink, he folds his elbows on the table and rests his chin on his fists.

"Something wrong?" I ask.

He exhales. "When I signed up, I was all Stars and Stripes. Now I see three years of mud and marching, being cannon fodder for strangers. If I had someone like you, a kind of big brother, it might be less frightening."

The room turns itself inside out. With Sam, I had to advise him against such bravado, but now I must build up whatever seedling of courage Pvt. George C. Hall has sprouting in his gifted head.

"Here in Company C, we are comrades in arms."

I sip my now-cold coffee, watching as my words pour over him. This youngster needs me as much as those horses and mules do, maybe more. God knows, war is hell, and I'm not leaving him alone in it. Responsibility is a confusing puzzle, but one you cannot simply abandon.

I'll tell Cpl. Starrott in the morning.

Chapter Five

By February, rumors are buzzing with the prospect of Ulysses Grant's being commissioned to advance upon two Confederate forts. If we take Ft. Henry on the Tennessee River and Ft. Donelson on the Cumberland, we open up access to Nashville and most of the state of Tennessee.

When the bugler finally calls us to action, we're packed aboard two steamboats and on the water within minutes. Soon, a turbulent storm pounds down upon us. The boats pitch like matchsticks in a giant eggbeater. As rain pounds the deck, I do my best to make sure I'm on the same steamboat as George.

Our 78th sails over mines planted in the Tennessee River to block us.

"They call 'em torpedoes," says our boat captain. "They must have leaked or something!"

Blanketed by the fog, Leggett loses sight of the second boat. We thrash and turn, but our helmsman cannot find it.

Hope it's not run aground!

After an hour and a half searching and calling, we finally locate it; it only cast anchor!

We sail directly past Ft. Henry's powder magazine, inundated by stormwater. It's abandoned. No rebels. No Yanks. Just dead Confederate soldiers sprawled in grotesque contortions along the riverbank. George is sickened at the sight. I can't blame him. He was already on tenterhooks from the missing boat, and it's our first brush with death outside of a funeral parlor.

———

The storm delays us significantly, but on February 16th, we finally make it to Ft. Donelson and Grant's Army of the Tennessee.

"Look! They're raising Old Glory over Donelson!" everyone exclaims. "The battle is won!"

Mortimer Leggett, now a colonel, assigns the bunch of us to protect our supply train and to take control of the prisoners. As we shackle them for rail transport to Northern prisons, a captured Confederate lieutenant by the name of Fairlane tells us the story of the battle we missed.

"Our leadin' Confederate General, Pierre Gustav Toutant Beauregard, our hero for bombin' your Ft. Sumpter and beating y'all at Bull Run, he was put in charge of defendin' Ft. Donelson by his boss, Albert Sidney Johnston. But from there on, things went downhill for us Confeds," he announces, while his rebel buddies in shackles are groaning and making grimaces of disgust.

"Beauregard begged off, y'see, claimin' a sore throat. He appointed John Floyd, fresh from failure in Virginia. Floyd launched a surprise attack, opening a hole in your Yankee line. But only Nathan Bedfort Forest's cavalry got through it. A couple of our spies infiltrated y'all's camp, and tried to warn Floyd when all of them gunboats started showin' up in the river, along with your new reserves coming down. But the messenger, he got lost somehow. Outnumbered, Floyd feared capture on account of facin' corruption charges in Washington and turned over his command to Gideon Pillow.

"Now Pillow, he already had been court-martialed for insubordination, see, and he passed the responsibility on to Simon Buckner, knowin' that Buckner had been a friend o' Grant's."

"Before the war," I surmise.

"Mexican War," Fairlane nods. "In the past, Buckner handed a drunken Grant, losin' his commission, a fistful o' travel money for goin' home to Ohio. But instead of goin' easy, Grant demanded unconditional surrender. U. S. Grant becomes Unconditional Surrender Grant!"

Grant is more complex than I had thought.

"What happened to Floyd and Pillow?" asks one of our boys.

"Well, both o' them lit out for Nashville by boat under the cover o' darkness."

Another prisoner adds, "My boy was ringin' the church bell. Rumors spread that the South had won, and they were celebratin'. The preacher, he's praisin' God for the victory until a man bursts in and shouts about how Yankee gunboats are a comin'!"

"How you know all that?" an infantryman asks.

"'Cause my boy skedaddled down here to tell me. That's b'fore you got us all by the ass!" the rebel snaps before turning to me. "Hey, buddy, ya got a buck?"

"I'd be in trouble giving you money."

As we board them onto the northbound train and wish them luck, I notice how thinly worn their boots are. They're just ordinary men like George and me—ill-equipped and slop-pily led by their generals.

And us? We're stuffing them into boxcars like bales of cotton!

As the locomotive hoots and pulls away, I stare after it. Isn't an army built on valor? Johnston passed off a duty to Beauregard. Beauregard to Floyd. Floyd to Pillow. Pillow to Buckner. And then, there was Grant. Couldn't he have been just a little more generous to the man who had rescued his reputation? Does any one of us really know what they're doing? Or do we just patch holes when they appear? My image of warriors is bold and fearless.

But if what that rebel said was true... What, indeed, is service?

One bright, hopeful star breaks through the gloom when we discover a rebel tied to a tree. Upon searching him, we discover that message that never got delivered, warning Floyd of our advance. He tells of a "deranged Indian" halting his horse and binding him to the tree. We realize it was our maverick Native ally, whom we affectionately call "Pasquale."

At night as I lie on my cot, I wonder what kind of generals would pass responsibility down the line four times? Why would a successful general like Ulysses S. Grant refuse leniency to an old friend?

The following morning, the bugler sounds mail call. When my name is called, the boys pass an envelope down the line to me. As I tear it open, shame creeps up my cheeks; I still haven't written Sam to thank him for taking my son under his wing.

757 Chestnut St., Zanesville, Ohio
February 2, 1862

My dear brother-in-law William,

Your son Johnny has been a joy in our household. His character of honesty is a joy. There are times when one can wish it weren't. There are circumstances related to your dear wife's passing that you deserve to know, and if I neglected to tell you, no one else would. Almost certainly, Mary's death was caused by a sudden and massive stroke. A few days ago, I asked Johnny to bring me some turmeric from the spice shelf and, being the helpful boy he is, he immediately gave me the jar, and said, "You know, Aunt Syd, before Mommy died, she wanted some sugar from the larder, but the sound of her words came out, "Please bring me some _Shubra_ from the _border_." And she talked funny in other ways, too. Once she looked straight at me and said, "Oh, how sweet! I see _two_ Johnnys!"

I got Sam from the sawmill, and we called on Dr. Phillips. He said the slurred speech and double vision were indicative of a severe hemorrhagic stroke and suggested Sam and I keep checking with Johnny to discern anything else.

After a few days, Johnny told us that when Mary collapsed, she asked him to: "Go find

Daddy, but how do you suppose she thought I could?"

I could only assure the boy that his mother loved him and was too sick to realize how things were.

William, I am not telling you this to disturb you. But you deserve to know. Johnny is functioning well in all respects; in fact, he is so articulate that I sometimes imagine him as a famous writer one day!

Stay well. Thank you for your service to the nation and its future.

Love always,
Sydney Laughlin

My breath freezes. I exhale and try to swallow around the lump in my throat. Then thunder strikes! She needed me, and I wasn't there! If I had not gone off, I could have observed her symptoms and reported them to the doctor. There was no one to blame but myself.

Upon reading the letter again, I fall to my knees. I could have saved her! She called for me!

"Go find Daddy!"

A thousand thoughts and possibilities echo in my head until I can't take it anymore. I bolt upright and run outside, sprinting through the compound with the sound of her cries echoing in my ears: Go! Go! Go find Daddy! No matter what the reason, the truth was she needed me, and I was not there.

Night comes. I don't notice. I sit on a keg of horseshoe nails, the letter limp in my hand. Will her cries ever cease?

By April, the shock is not abating. Days pass in fog and fever before I can feel my feet beneath me again, as we hit the trail through the woods, marching toward Dover. Mile after mile, boots trudge along, and our carriage wheels squeak. The reins in my hands are useless. No matter what I do, my mind is still lost in the terror Johnny must have felt that night. I flop down on dry leaves only to be met with a downpour at midnight. No new food wagon replaces our stock. We are wet and cold from tramping through the mud. The next day, each man only receives half the ration they should have. By the second sunrise, only a third, and by day three, there's nothing left. Unfortunately, a wagoner belongs halfway to the Quartermaster Corps. His other half belongs to his military unit.

Men offer a single hard-tack cracker for five dollars. We wait for further orders from Grant. He's over by the river at Pittsburgh Landing.

Eventually, the rain stops. Mary's cries don't. We pitch tents on the only level ground in Dover, an area that had been used by the Confederates as a shallow burying ground. Men fall ill from the stench of the dead faster than Surgeon Reeves and Chaplain Todd can handle. Even Col. Leggett succumbs to the stench! If we did have food, it wouldn't stay down...

Bodies pile up faster than we can ship them home. Word spreads of Dr. Thomas Holmes' developing an embalming process by studying Egyptian mummy heads. Lincoln himself had it applied to the body of his friend, Col. Elmer Ellsworth.

Impressed with the results, he ordered the process to become standard for all Union dead. But none of that makes the constant shroud of gloom any easier to wade through.

Eventually, we discover that Dover has an industrial plant

for Confederate artillery and demolish it. The surrounding shacks are abandoned, but the residents tell us they once belonged to slaves who escaped aboard trains or joined the Yankee march passing through. We salvage the remains of what little food we can find, and all the while, the stories of those families never leave my thoughts.

Soon, we move on to Metal Landing. George Richey in Company A falls ill. He is treated and sent to recover, only to return to the regiment rather than accepting the offered furlough. A few days later. He dies from a disease contracted in the filth of Dover.

Disease and desertion claim far more men than bullets.

Leggett appoints me Supply Master of the combined military materiel. The next morning, one of my lead horses staggers. Somebody tried to poison him. When I ask around, George says he saw a bluecoat from the 124th Illinois Infantry lurking about in the campfire light. That regimen is known for careless supervision. One of their men, Pvt. Hiram Castleberry, even keeps a pet pig.

I commend George for his observation, "You could run spy missions for the Bureau of Military Information."

Before leaving Metal Landing, Cpl. Starrott brings a complaint before the JAG Corps officer against a certain Pvt. Castleberry, but despite George's testimony, he was let off on grounds of insufficient evidence. According to George, Castleberry left the hearing wearing a wide smirk. There was no further mention of the pig.

Chapter Six

A few days later. Leggett orders some drills to keep us sharp.

When we assemble, his voice booms across the camp. "Gentlemen! We move out at sundown, eastward! Ready and in formation in sixty. We've got a bridge to burn for our Southern hosts."

Excitement runs through the regiment. My muscles and senses snap to attention. Is this a battle?

Quick as I can, I call down through the supply train, "Wagons! Water and ready eastward in sixty!" My comrades echo the command down a line of twenty wagons.

An hour later my wagon is packed beyond the buckboard; I'm mounted on the left horse of the wheel pair of the team.

We move out in silence until Leggett calls out, "Stealth, boys. No random shooting, even if the rattlesnakes get on your path."

Our wagons are noisy. The timbers creak, the wheels squeal, and the cargo shifts, but the horses and mules pour them along as faithfully and quietly as they can. They don't even snort despite the downing mist drifting through the moon's silver beams. We go two miles. Then three.

"Halt!" Leggett signals above his head. I gently pull on the reins as the rest of the line comes to a stop. The ordinance team scrambles over the rocks leading to the bridge, tools strapped to their belts.

Singing and caroling echo through the air from the Confederate camp nearby. Campfire smoke swirls in the breeze. It's a small group, perhaps only one company.

Please don't see us, I pray silently as we march forward. I don't know what they'll do if they come after us.

The ordnance team empties packs stuffed with wood shavings under the bridge trestles. Coal oil follows, poured. Everyone backs away. One man whips out a percussion cap, draws his flintlock pistol. It glimmers in the moonlight. He touches flame to the wick and *woosh.*

Fire dances upward, singeing branches, fanned by the breeze, lighting the night sky with a roar that echoes down the canyon, bright as an Independence Day celebration. That bridge is out of commission.

Rebel tents collapse, and cooking pots are abandoned. Their ammunition wagon is stuck in the mud. A knot of men strain and grunt, trying to shove it away from the advancing flame.

We barely make it back to Adamsville camp and catch the twinkle of a snooze before, in a noontime downpour, galloping hooves break the quiet.

A rider bursts into view: blue jacket, not gray. A Union quartermaster dismounts, breathless. "General Wallace! A message for General Lew Wallace from General Ulysses Grant."

Gen. Wallace rides up. "Well? News from Pittsburgh Landing?"

The man is soaked through. He stammers between gasps. "Grant's been pushed...from Shiloh Church...into the oaks... called Hornets' Nest... Albert Sidney Johnston and his CSA rebels, some 45,000, broke into the camp before dawn, and even...bayonetted...some men while they slept. Grant needs your division...fast."

"You've carried his orders? You must have them in writing."

"He didn't write them...just told me to get here damned fast...and if you want them, I'm to write them."

"Christ, man! You know we don't do that! An imposter could ride in here and give verbal commands!" Wallace yanks a map from his pack. "There are two roads to Pittsburgh Landing. Did he say which road brings us into his left flank?"

"No, sir."

"Then you buck-saddle eight miles back to Grant and tell him we're coming, and on the Shunpike Road."

The quartermaster snaps a salute. "Sir!"

He wheels his horse left. Hooves fling tufts of mud behind him as he breaks into a gallop.

We start out, slogging through rotten weather with pride. Does Grant even know what he's doing? I'm again astride the left wheel horse, cold, dampness creeping through my saddle. It must be soaking through the foot soldiers' worn-thin boots. Creaking, swishing, sloshing, men and animals in one long, miserable pull.

A couple of miles later, another rider gallops toward us. What now? He pushes through to Gen. Wallace and salutes.

"Col. Rowley, sir! Gen. Grant's division has been forced into a new defensive position! Their backs are against the river! He says come with all speed, or they could all be in it!"

"Hand me those orders," Wallace demands, impatient. "You can observe, we're already moving."

"I do not have written orders, sir."

"What's become of army regulations?" Wallace roars. "The Devil might have his day, but we will be there at all hazards when we can be there."

Without a word, the colonel wheels around and breaks into a trot.

A few miles farther, a black man bursts from the trees, soaked through, dressed in rags, and plants himself in the road. He waves his arms and presses a finger to his mouth.

Please trust him, Wallace. The black folks have been our allies.

"Easy, man." Wallace's voice turns firm but soft as he swings his palm back to halt the march. "What information do you bear?"

The man shakes, then chokes out, "There's a Confederate battalion on the road. It's straight ahead, over the next hill."

"You're certain?"

"I am. Sure as God made little green apples. They 'bout caught me 'fore I ran."

Wallace pulls a hardtack biscuit from his vest and hands it to him. "Countermarch, gentlemen. We're crossing over to the River Road."

I lean back in the saddle, brush rainwater off my face, and take a long breath. Extending the march with a countermarch is trial enough in this weather. But reversing direction with a supply train of twenty wagons? In mud? A wagoner's nightmare. Sweat runs down into my beard. The sun begins to set. We won't reach Pittsburgh Landing before dark.

Tired and huffing, we reach Grant's left flank, exhausted. It's seven p.m. by my pocket watch.

The first day's fighting is over, and the casualties remain unknown. We're told Albert Sidney Johnston took a shot to the back of his right knee, fell off his horse, and bled to death in his boot. The story makes no sense to us. An officer leading troops is generally in front of them. A shot in the back of Johnston's knee would have to come from his own side.

But there's no time to dwell on contradictions. We have to keep moving, or the panorama of dead and wounded will turn our legs and will to mush.

Despite losing Gen. Johnston, with the Yanks locked in at the Hornets' Nest, the rebels think they've won the day. Their celebration carries through the night. Pvt. Szewzyski, always inquisitive, volunteers to investigate. He finds a drunken rebel stumbling from camp and asks what's going on. The man, not realizing he's speaking to an enemy, laughs.

"Ha! We're eatin' cake and toastin' ourselves with bourbon mixed with gunpowder!" Then he turns aside and empties his stomach into the woods.

Overnight, Don Carlos Buell's Army of the Ohio arrives from Nashville. Union strength swells to 65,000 against their 45,000 on day two. Every one of us is determined to fight all day without stopping to eat.

Our 78th Ohio Infantry leads the attack to the front of Pittsburgh Landing, joined by the 1st Illinois Light Artillery. The bugle calls "Fix bayonets," and a shiver runs down my spine, through my gut, and into my feet. A bayonet means driving steel through a man's body. It means summoning the kind of courage that bites at a moral conscience and still gets demanded by the moment. George is shaken, stuck on the image of men bayonetted in their sleep.

Sweating, he hesitates to raise his bayonet while shots and

shells stream overhead. I grab the back of his neck and shove him down to evade a hit. Both men in blue and gray fall. The battle rages between town and a whitewashed Methodist log church named, with cruel irony, "Shiloh," while the smell of death, so familiar now, invades our nostrils once more.

A musket ball scrapes through the flesh of my left thigh. I've just finished reloading. I fire and hit my assailant, a huge hulk of a man ambling forward, his right arm damaged. He growls profanities as he coils on the grass. His comrades rush in and drag him away, shrilling threats over their shoulders:

"You hit Big Cyrus Braddox! No one ever hits Big Cyrus and lives! You're a dead man, you damned Yankee!"

I don't know if I should fear Braddox or expect never to see him again. But if I hadn't fired, my military career would've ended right there. And though he's gone, I need to be watchful for whichever division of the Confederate army this monstrous, hulking man came from.

My eyes follow the panicked band as they retreat across the field. As they do, I see a fallen man not far away on the murky ground, one of our best allies, known for tricks that foil the rebels. He's the guerrilla fighter who tied their messenger to a tree at Ft. Donelson. Tall and skinny maverick, Lakota Sioux has a vendetta against the CSA for killing his two children. His Lakota name is Pas-qua-thalu, but we all affectionately call him "Pasquale." His left leg hangs, shattered by a rebel canister shot.

At the sight of such a loyal fighter disabled, I scramble over, lift him over my shoulder, and carry him through shells piercing the damp air. At the hospital tent, I plead for triage, and the doctors spring into action. With a man like him, you don't hesitate.

Surgeon Reeves performs the only procedure that can save his life: amputation.

"I see you need some dressing as well," another doctor says.

I touch the thigh he indicates. It's slick with blood. He applies dressing and bandages. It's my first acquaintance with the fact that human urine is sterile and can be used as an antiseptic in battle. I hadn't even remembered my wound as I carried Pasquale. My only concern was ensuring he stayed alive.

Is this what real service is?

Two of our navy's ironclad gunboats on the Tennessee River assist in the attack. By 3:00 p.m. the second day, Beauregard retreats toward Corinth. Our company pursues the fleeing rebels beyond Corinth to Bethel.

Shiloh is a Union victory, but newspapers erupt over the report of casualties, blaming the large numbers on our late arrival under Wallace. Grant's wrongly dispatched verbal commands rage in my head.

Dismayed, Henry Halleck removes Grant from field command and demotes him to a secondary position while making himself commander of the Western Theater. Grant blames Wallace for "failure to obey orders" and "taking the wrong road." He admits to nothing about giving only verbal orders twice. Neither does he credit Wallace for the second-day combat, without which the losses would've been far worse. Our moral fiber is fraying. And it's obvious the guilt he didn't earn is weighing heavily on Wallace.

Restless, I go to check on George. At the telegraphy tent, I overhear that the King of Siam wishes to ship war elephants to assist our cause, and Lincoln has diplomatically refused.

I continue to camp to tell George about the elephants and ask how he fared. He's silent, writing a letter.

"Have you heard about Jim Morton?" he asks at last, without looking up.

"From Zanesville," I reply. "What happened?"

He lifts his head. "He took a shot and died within minutes. That's Company C's first battle casualty."

Chapter Seven

Soon, it's time to root out the "Vertebrae of the Confederacy," Corinth, Beauregard's base of operations. Corinth has the only rail line connecting the Mississippi River with the Atlantic Ocean. If we can take Corinth, we seriously weaken their mobility and have a shot at Vicksburg on the Mississippi.

Henry Halleck, now general-in-chief, organizes our 78th Ohio, with Lew Wallace's army, to lay a siege around Corinth. Halleck employs a tactic he used fifteen years ago in Mexico, advancing at a slow pace and fortifying each day's advance, moving only five miles in three weeks. So, on the dawn of April 29th, our Union troops wake up to the roar of cannons, as the rebels open a charge so suddenly, the Federals are caught entirely off guard!

Our job is to protect the Union's right flank by guarding the road leading out of Corinth. Reinforcements are ordered in, including forty untrained mules, which delays our arrival until 9:00 p.m.

As we finally close in, the rebels begin to retreat.

Thousands are taken prisoner. Munitions lay scattered on the road, along with blankets and the customary playing cards. Gambling is not permitted, so fleeing soldiers often abandon their playing cards.

The 1st Illinois Light Artillery, famed at Shiloh, places a battery on a cliff overlooking the wooded area. A group of us goes out in the woods, and if we spot rebels, we give a signal.

We hear them before we see them; their commander is giving a speech.

"Sons of the South, we are here to defend our homes, our wives and children against the hordes of vandals who have come to possess this sacred soil. Is there a man so base among those who hear me, as to retreat from the contemptible foe? I will never blanch before their fire, nor…"

We give our signal, and six shells find their mark. The officer and his troop scatter.

The next morning, all our Yankee divisions plus our gunboats on the river break forth. The enemy is sent into complete disorder, but they fight. We settle into the siege and bombard them. Casualties climb from battle and disease. Outbreaks of both typhoid and "the bloody flux" (dysentery) take many. Col. Leggett's horse is shot. He's thrown but survives.

The siege stretches through May. On the evening of the 29th, our men find a flowing artesian well. Everyone strips and bathes, not caring that we're polluting the Corinth citizens' water source.

Something tells me there's a message hidden in this water.

When I return to my ammo wagon, I find my lead horses' trace and bridle have been disturbed. I jump up on the hitch and take a look inside. There, curled up among the cartridge boxes, lies a soldier! He's wearing the insignia of the 90th Illinois Infantry.

"What's this?" I bellow. "Who are you?"

The soldier climbs out and stands with a salute. "Pvt. Frank Miller, sir, 90th Illinois." He's sweating profusely and holding his stomach. Common symptoms of the dysentery prevalent among the men.

"Got the bloody flux?" I ask. "Is that why you didn't bathe in the stream with all the other fellas?"

"No," says Frank, standing up. "It's this!" and he jerks open his jacket and pulls up his shirt to showcase a highly feminine figure. My stomach drops. Her courage astounds me, but if she's caught, she'll be dead. After a few failed attempts, I sputter out the only question I can muster.

"So...who are you really?"

She straightens and buttons her uniform. "Franny-Liz, er... Frances Elizabeth Quinn, sir! Seventeen years old, LaMoille, Bureau County, Illinois."

A fellow Midwesterner. And she's pretty. "At ease, ma'am. I'm William Laughlin. Glad to meet you." I hold my chin up and give a perfunctory salute. "How the dickens did you get into the army?"

"My brother Tommy and I were both orphaned in our teens," she says. "We each were placed with different family relatives. Tommy ran away when he was fourteen and enlisted in the army. I was put in a convent in Virginia, but I wanted to serve my country. I went to Chicago and enlisted in the 90th Illinois under an alias."

I touch her forehead. It's hot; fever hot.

"Franny-Liz, if we don't get you to Surgeon Reeves fast, they'll be carrying you to the train on a stretcher!"

Frances pleads, "That's a chance I have to take! If they find out I'm a woman, they'll put me on the train." She falls to her knees.

Does she know what that's doing to me? Now she's looking up at me from below. Not in weakness, but intensively.

"I entreat you, sir! Let me stay a few more days. Just hold my secret for a few days and see if I don't get better!" She drops her head.

I kneel and study her face. The soft blueness of her eyes reminds me so much of Mary. They hold her same quiet resilience. And in that moment, I can't refuse her. I stand. "Okay. Deal."

I lift up the tarp shielding the cartridge boxes in the wagon and drape it over her. Then brush my team down and check their hooves, making every effort to keep my hands busy while my mind swirls with thoughts of Franny's secret—and how long I can keep her alive.

Footsteps traipse through the mud. I spin around and squint through the haze. Is it? ... How can it be? ... Hiram Castleberry wanders casually around the wagon, studying the shape of the tarp, and not looking in my direction. My neck begins to sweat.

After a few moments, I stride up to him.

He's still staring at the tarp. He draws his pistol and taps its handle against the sideboard, "D'you always protect an' cover up your cargo this much? I heard a little shuffling last night, and saw a shadow slippin' in beside your load. Maybe one of your mares with the colic." He blows his nose in his hand and wipes it across his beard.

I grip the side of the wagon. My fingertips brush the tarp. I feel not a ripple, thank God!

He turns away, but gives me a side glance over his shoulder, furrowing his brow, just long enough to make me feel uncomfortable, then growls, "Ain't none o' my business anyhow... unless it gets to be."

A choking lump jams in my throat. He ambles off without another word. I remain motionless until he is out of range.

"All clear!" I whisper toward the tarp.

"Phew!" She reaches out. I take her hand gently. The fingers are thin, but her hand is graced with the roughness of farm labor. I don't know if she wants me to hold her hand or to hold her. I must not allow myself to be too forward. She grips my hand firmly.

I squeeze back. "That man Castleberry is up to no good," I caution. "Better get back to your unit before bed count. Find me if you need me." Something is fascinating about this woman. Her bravery? Her resolve? Or, perhaps, simply her attractiveness. I turn and start walking toward my waiting team of wagon horses.

She climbs out, comes up behind me, and gives me a hug, kissing the back of my neck. "I'm thirsty. You got any water?"

She didn't get into the artesian stream when the rest of us did. "All I've got is in the horse pail hanging from the back axle. From all the regiment's bathing dirt."

"Good enough," she answers, heading toward the rear of the wagon.

I draw a deep breath, trying to calm the sick feeling that Castleberry might be watching, that he might have been watching for days. I go back to brushing my horses and talk to them gently, loud enough for her to hear.

But when I turn around, she's not at the wagon. She's not at the water pail. She's gone.

Chapter Eight

Atrain whistles over the Mobile-Ohio depot where Beauregard and his rebels are holding camp. Wild cheers rise from their lines and drill sergeants bark commands.

Are they planning a morning assault?

The sounds settle into bugle calls and drum rolls. Campfire smoke drifts and dances in the air. The quiet returns, but sleep does not come easily for us.

Before dawn, our sentry team goes to investigate and returns with their report. "They're gone! Marched out through the night! Their artillery and supplies must've been loaded on the outbound train carrying their sick and wounded."

Frances. She needs a different train, a different medical team. Should I have been more forceful? What if dysentery humiliates her before it kills her? My jaw tightens until my teeth ache. She's been a good soldier. Don't I owe a comrade at arms?

The arrival of new captees; a skeleton crew left behind to tend the fires and keep up the drums and bugles to throw us off. Wooden decoy "Quaker guns" sit on their line. The crew surrenders and tells us that Beauregard slipped away to Tupelo.

"Hey, Laughlin! Your buddy Hall's in sick bay with a fever!"

Have I been away from George too long? "Thanks," I toss over my shoulder, and run for the hospital tent.

George is distraught, convinced he's got typhoid or dysentery. I go straight to Surgeon Reeves. Thankfully, George has neither typhoid nor dysentery. Just a nasty respiratory condition after breathing sulfurous black smoke from rifles and cannons.

Most of the men celebrate Corinth with pilfered local bourbon. I can't. Concern for Frances keeps me roaming Corinth's emptied streets. The only business still open is a druggist's.

He looks up from his ledger. "Ya think you Yanks can hold Corinth?"

"That's to be seen," I answer.

He rams his quill into the inkwell. "If the South can't hold Corinth, she probably can't hold any other place, and ain't worth defendin'."

I nod.

The druggist studies me. "Now, you're 78th Ohio, ain't you? You know any fellows from the 90th Illinois by chance?" He makes a slow circle in the air with his finger.

My breath catches. Frances. Play dumb. "Uh...why do you ask?"

The druggist blushes. "Seemed unusual is all. A young soldier came in this mornin'. Wore 90th Illinois insignia. Had a young negro girl with him askin' for medicine to relieve menstrual cramps. Girl had a little black baby strapped to her back."

I squint and pull my mouth to one side. "Did you help them?"

"No. Don't want trouble with runaway slaves an' all." He shrugs. " I had my assistant run and tell one of the 90th's officers." He stops. "Hey, you ain't an inspector, are yuh?"

I mutter a hurried goodbye and hit the road out of town.

What is Frances doing with a black woman and a baby?

I stop at a cotton field. A group of African women work the rows, and one lies collapsed, face-down in the dirt.

They call to me. "Not to worry! The lady fell from sunstroke. But if you the soldier lookin' for her daughter and baby, they took their chances and went to the contraband camp just east outside o' Corinth."

As I approach the makeshift camp, panting, I catch wind of a forceful male voice, answered by a gentle but steady female one. Frances. She must have found a kind of shelter here.

I enter and see a lieutenant questioning her as she sits on a stool, which might as well be a witness stand. I announce myself. "Pvt. William Laughlin, sir. 78th Ohio."

Frances looks up. She tells the officer she needed medicine for cramping, but didn't dare ask the druggist while impersonating a man. "I didn't know how I would get any," she says, then leaves the stool and wraps her arms around me. "But then I came across this girl in a cotton field holding a baby."

"That was me," a teenage girl breaks in. "I'm Jamie. The baby's Andrew, my brother. Our mama passed out pickin' cotton, and this soldier offered to take the child to a black folks' settlement, but I first went with her to the drug store. That's when I found out the soldier was really a woman." She lifts her chin. "I said, sure thing. I knew my baby brother'd be cared for." She points, proud. "He's right over there." In the corner, a middle-aged black woman smiles and rocks the baby against her breast.

The lieutenant blinks hard, almost undone. His face works through indecision.

"Thanks for coming," Frances says softly to me. "It's okay. They'll finally be putting me on the train, just like you said." Then, in a whisper, "Please...see me off on the morning train. God bless you."

I snap to attention, both because the lieutenant is watching and because my body needs something strict to hold on to.

"Col. Leggett has been apprised of the incident," the officer says crisply. "You can expect to be hearing from him."

Out of the frying pan and into the fire.

Chapter Nine

Henry Halleck has finally undone himself! Lincoln is outraged because Beauregard was allowed to escape. Halleck has been "kicked upstairs" to Washington to become chief of staff in the War Department. Lincoln perceives him as "little more than a first-class clerk." The president is now looking for a new general-in-chief.

I'm not sure at all what I have won, except maybe disciplinary action from Col. Leggett. The march to his office is like being thrown in the guardhouse, or worse! Suddenly, cheers erupt throughout the camp.

Grant's back in command of the Mississippi River basin! It's the first good news we've had in weeks. And to make matters even better, newspapers are publishing Lincoln's declaration regarding giving Grant back his command. A cheer rises from the men, echoing Lincoln's words: "I can't spare this man, he fights!"

True enough. For all his faults, Grant belongs on the fields; he is uniquely dedicated, and his enthusiasm is shared with the men around him.

Grant makes Corinth his base of operation and amasses his troops in the city's Tippan Square, 40,000 of them, with his eyes on Vicksburg. Rebel forces return the favor by tearing up the railroad tracks between Corinth and Vicksburg. Our men are assigned to repair their damage, supervised by one of the greatest, Gen. William Tecumseh Sherman, affectionately known as "Cump," or "Uncle Bill." Soon, he intends to advance upon LaGrange to take over a Confederate supply base.

For now, on the northbound Mobile-Ohio line, I've volunteered to help board civilians without property onto rail cars to escape conscription. The sick and wounded are being loaded as well. I think of Frances. She needs to be on this train. Will I find her here at the depot? Still nothing from Leggett. When does the axe fall?

Someone wraps their arms around me from behind. I turn. "You're good at that."

She blushes, courtsies, and meets my eyes. "You came."

I shift my weight. "Of course. Is this...just goodbye?"

"It's to tell you," she says, holding me tighter, "that I'm grateful." Then she plants a wet kiss on my bearded cheek. "And I hope they don't come down hard on you for helping me."

"If they do, chalk it up to happenstance," I say, still holding her. "You'll remain an admirable woman." I pause. Dare I ask? "What's next? Home to LaMoille for treatment? Will you write me?"

"I'll get treated," she says brightly, "and all that feminine nonsense." She grins. "Then I'll enlist again, under a new regiment with a new name." She mimics tightening a bow tie. "Edgar? Montmorency? Theophilus?" We laugh.

I pause. "And if you're discovered?"

"If they remove me again, I'll find another unit. If I'm taken prisoner, I'll break out. I promise." She shadowboxes the air. "Nothing's stopping me from serving my country."

I can't help smiling. "You should be one of our generals. You'll do good in this war."

We walk to the nearest railcar, kicking loose pebbles. The locomotive shrieks.

"Time to go," she says. A quick lip-smack. A tap on my shoulder. She mounts the step.

"Goodbye," I say, releasing her hand. "God bless you. Write between your military engagements."

"Sure will, my buddy."

She's gone.

The Mobile-Ohio lurches forward, smoke swallowing the platform and my sudden emptiness. Frances will heal, disguise herself again, and move on. Me? I've lost yet another dear friend. What's the cure for that?

"You all right, soldier?" a voice calls. The cloying scent of perfume coats the air.

I don't need a prostitute. I turn away, nearly tripping over a sleeping vagrant, and start walking. Anywhere.

Frances Quinn showed me the stamina women carry. Like Mary. Like my sisters. Gentle on the surface. Enduring underneath. The lesson steels me to face an enemy like Braddox. I wonder if I'll ever see Frances again.

As we move toward LaGrange, my sense of loss folds into a new one. Supplies overflow, but food for man and beast runs short. I send wagons out daily to forage. The townspeople give what they can: fruit, berries. A baker hands over fresh bread. LaGrange yields by June 13th without a shot being fired.

Not everyone here is friendly. I read editorials condemning abolitionists, twisted and venomous. It reminds me that even Ohio is split.

With fighting slowed, boredom frays tempers. Buglers and

drummers lose their edge. Talk turns petty, whose regiment is better. Col. Leggett announces a drill contest for diversion, to be held on August 23rd. Four officers draw names; three judges, one presenter. The prize: a new U.S. flag. Wagering begins and is kept hidden from the brass.

The drills are brutal. When finalists are named, my stomach tightens. Our 78th Ohio is pitted against the 124th Illinois. Castleberry's regiment.

On a plateau outside town, a ring is marked. Townsfolk crowd in. Children perch on shoulders. Lemonade carts roll through. Even war needs spectacle.

We go first. Our movements are sharp and clean. Loud cheers ascend from the crowd.

The 124th Illinois goes next. The applause thins. As they clear the field, Castleberry stalks past me and hisses, "We've got you beat, you Buckeye bastards." A little girl glances up at her father, who is scowling in disapproval. Castleberry sneers again. My mind flashes to the wagon, the tarp, his warning; that what was under there was none of his business. Unless it gets to be.

What does he know?

Before I can dwell on that too long, the judges confer. Two from Illinois vote for the 124th. The crowd barely reacts. The third, an Iowan, votes for us. Cheers erupt. Someone behind us mutters, "Something crooked's afloat."

At the presentation, the designated officer refuses to award the flag, declaring the decision unjust.

Who is this Castleberry? What does he know of my secret? He's been in the spotlight against me ever since I was promoted to Supply Master. Is it jealousy? And how do we explain, for God's sake, the corruption, now so obvious to all, that two judges from his state freely compromise honesty? And why? It's a nasty thought, but I secretly hope that their rations run out and they eat that ridiculous pig Bowser that Castleberry keeps.

There's still no word from Leggett. Why is he stringing me out?

Outside town, we encounter a refugee camp larger than Corinth's. I search for Jamie and little Andrew, wondering if they're safe. Starrott says Grant has sworn to support such contraband settlements throughout the basin.

"Why are they called 'contraband'?" someone asks.

"That term is credited to Gen. Benjamin Butler," he says. "Butler reasoned that, since the ownership of negroes is not sanctioned by the United States, receiving them was equivalent to confiscating contraband. He has an odd way of classifying persons."

"Sounds like a conniving officer."

Starrott recounts Butler's Women's Proclamation in New Orleans. The story chills me.

"When Butler governed New Orleans, one female resident dumped a full chamber pot on the head of Adm. Farragut. Butler posted his notorious Women's Proclamation, 'Any woman showing contempt for Union personnel shall be held liable to be treated as a woman of the town plying her avocation.'"

I pause. "How could Butler have been permitted to enact such a vengeful edict?"

"Henry Halleck relocated him," Starrott replies. "An odd bird, all right, disposed to riding at night in his bedroom slippers, reciting poetry."

I ask George what he thinks.

"He's downright misogynistic," George says. "A real man doesn't degrade a woman, no matter the provocation."

He's right.

I thank Starrott and walk George to a bench in Grand Junction Memorial Park. He confesses his fear of returning home without a sweetheart.

"I don't have one either," I say quietly, "but one found me."

He nearly somersaults. "Who?"

I swallow a laugh. "Do you know a private in the 90th Illinois, Frank Miller? He is really a woman, Frances Elizabeth Quinn. Before I say more, you must pledge secrecy." George collects himself from the grass and stares at me.

"You've got it, as sure as our pact at Camp Gilbert."

"Okay. Frances came to hide in my wagon load when all the men stripped naked and jumped into that artesian stream like so many schoolboys. And I'm not just tantalizing you, George. I might need your assistance protecting her secret."

I extend a hand. A grin splits his face as he shakes it.

"Come on, let's take a walk around the refugee camp and see if the folks are all right!"

Chapter Ten

"If you would like to come and supervise the work of the plantation, honey, you can have whatever you ask!" The breathy invitation is delivered from a young Southern belle in tight trousers and a peasant blouse. She's running her fingers through the red hair of the 2nd Lieutenant of Company E, at a plantation on Sagemeyer Road.

Brace yourself, William.

We were on a foraging detail on August 28th, in Bolivar, Tennessee. Dangerous territory, both for military transport purposes and my morality.

Whatever transpired between the lieutenant and this seductress, he would not disclose, but George and I heard men often gather more than food on a foraging run. "Wow," says George, "she is beautiful!"

"Yes, George. And she looks like a trap." I keep my voice low. "Look how she overdoes the come-on. Go easy. You'll find the right lady one day."

We travel on to an adjacent plantation, an orchard bespangled with peach trees. The fragrance alone sharpens my hunger for a lavish meal or any meal not boiled over a campsite fire. No time to pick. Where do they store the harvest?

An out shed full of crates stacked neatly as bricks.

We load enough to fill a wagon.

With a second wagon waiting, we scout for more. Behind a fenced bin draped with burlap sits a heap of watermelons. We crack one open and pass the dripping pieces through the crew. Sweet juices drip down our wrists under a darkening sky. Squatting in the dirt, we devour like boys, and through the cool air come the cracked tones of a piano.

Is this a war?

A young woman, wealthy by her fluttering hoop skirt and dangling jewelry, steps out of the farmhouse. "You fellas look mighty hungry. Why don't y'all come in? We ladies got a roast in the oven, ready in 'bout twenty minutes. After your watermelon appetizer, y'all come on in and 'lax y'selves."

My attention snaps to George for any sign of temptation. His interest is plain.

He leans toward me. "What's an all-dolled-up belle doing in a farmhouse?"

"If you're hungry, we'll find out what she's doing," our lieutenant says. "But be careful. Don't accept liquor. We don't know their motive. Maybe they want military information. Maybe they're offering sex for money. A drunken head could give away our location and empty your pockets at the same time."

I couldn't have warned George better myself.

The candlelight dinner is delicious. Roast beef. Okra stewed with tomatoes. Cornbread. Peach cobbler for dessert. Three women serve us, skirts whispering as they move about the kitchen. No men. No slaves. Half a dozen half-naked toddlers crawl and tumble across the floor. Conscription and self-manumission have stripped this place down to women and children, and whatever elegance they can still wear.

Stomachs full, we crowd the overstuffed Victorian satin furniture in the parlor. The women entertain us with Southern folk songs, with the piano accompanying from the corner.

Applause breaks out when the last song ends. The short, thin piano player, the one George can't stop watching, stands, courtsies, and says, "Now you boys don't have to scurry off. Y'all can stay as long as you like."

The lieutenant smiles, gracious, but his eyes stay sharp. "Thank you, ladies. Your dinner and your entertainment were first-class. We must collect forage for our horses and get back to our unit." A tiny jerk of his head toward the door sends us moving.

"Best seasoned hay is in the back!" the piano player calls as we file out.

George jabs me with his elbow. "But she invited—"

"Doesn't matter, George."

Outside, we hitch up to leave with two loaded wagons. One stacked with peaches. One with watermelons and the "best seasoned hay" for horses and mules. Tonight, the men will eat like kings.

George climbs onto the buckboard beside me. I keep my eyes forward. "Didn't mean to snap. Any one of them could be a spy. Any one of them could be playing the whore." I swallow and lower my voice. "The one you want might be innocent. These women lose men every day, men who don't come back. Maybe she's looking for a husband." I glance at him. "Hold it in your mind, buddy, consorting with the enemy is a serious infraction."

"How serious?"

I search for an example. "Remember Capt. Sinclair? Docked two months' pay for teaching a LaGrange boy to load a musket. Didn't know the kid was running a secesh spying mission."

"But what if she's not an enemy? That wouldn't be consorting with the enemy."

"Depends on what the judge decides when you're reviewed."

George goes quiet, eyes forward like he's studying a poker hand. Then he turns, palms open in a pleading gesture. "I kept a secret for you. You can keep a secret for me."

He has a point. I think of Frances. But still...

"George, we've had a deal. You asked me to shield you from danger. That outranks any secret."

He presses his thumb to his chin, staring ahead. I wait for it to settle into him.

We make our way back to camp. The men barely have time to enjoy peaches and watermelon before Leggett sends us to block the Van Buren Road leading to the Bolivar depot. Wiping juice from our mouths as we march, we spot WANTED posters nailed to trees, issued by CSA Gen. Earl Van Dorn. A $500 reward for Col. Leggett.

The Zanesville boys laugh. "No small achievement for a schoolmaster from Ohio!"

I feel my stomach go cold. If I hide, will there be posters for me?

We tear down some of the posters, and from the woods a small cluster of black men approaches Leggett, faces warm with urgency and alarm. The leader waves his straw hat. Leggett halts and waits as the man steps up. He's clean, bright-eyed, and barefoot.

"You have information about the CSA?"

"Yes, suh. Just five miles down the road yonder," he points, "they's a whole division with three generals; Armstrong, Price, and Van Dorn."

"Much obliged," Leggett says, then turns sharply to us. His hand jabs forward. "Company C and Company E, reconnaissance! Location! Size! Weaponry! Terrain!"

Their report confirms a concentration of rebel forces, and their commanders were named correctly. Confident we hold the road, Leggett sends a telegraph for reinforcement from Col. Force's 20th Ohio. Then, without waiting, he orders, "Charge!"

The fight surges back and forth along the Van Buren Road. Lt. Col. Harvey Hogg arrives and meets their assault at a cross-road with four infantry units, driving the enemy into retreat. Horses and rebel bodies litter the road.

Then, behind us, an unexpected cavalry force advances.

Leggett bellows to Hogg, "If you have any doubts about holding your position, draw back!"

Hogg shouts back, "For God's sake, don't order me back!"

"Meet them with charge, then, Colonel...and may Heaven bless you!"

I watch, awed, as Hogg reverses direction and roars, "Forward!" He rides to the front, saber flashing, shouting, "Give them cold steel, boys!" A stream of musket balls hits him. He drops hard to the ground.

How fast courage rises. How fast it's cut down.

His sacrifice should fortify our cause, this battle, and beyond. His valor can't be questioned, but I can't stop thinking about the bodies that fall after a man's bravery lights the fuse.

Capt. Musser of the 2nd Illinois cavalry takes over. Van Dorn charges our C and E companies. When Col. Force finally arrives, our combined force drives the rebels into an open field and surrounds them. We capture almost all of them, with only a few escaping.

Back in camp, the smell of campfire is a mercy compared to the battlefield's acrid stink. Company E has returned before us. They must've had no news of Company C, because when we stagger across the encampment threshold, swamp mud on our faces, bandages seeping, they leap up with a bellow of cheers and applause.

"A toast to C-Team!" Bottles appear and get passed.

When we settle, they ask, "How'd you get through?"

"A negro man guided Col. Wiles," someone answers. "Led us through ravines and channels, escape paths around Bolivar."

The revelry runs late.

Afterward, the Bolivar aftermath is handled in an orderly fashion. The Union grants protection to Southerners who take Lincoln's Oath of Allegiance. A wealthy planter named McNeal takes the oath to check his plantation. The next day, we catch him in full Confederate uniform as a major. A Presbyterian pastor takes the oath and our boys worship in his church. Other clergymen refuse, and they're piled into rail cars bound for northern prisons to "correct their insanity."

A short lull brings the postal carrier. "Mail call!" I'm thrilled to receive a letter from home.

757 Chestnut St.
Zanesville, Ohio
July 27, 1862

Dear William,

Sam and I hope this letter finds you active and well. I must tell you: young Johnny tried out for a part in a school play for the part of Robin Hood. He wants to be seen as the swashbuckling hero he sees in his father. Instead, the teacher recognized his gentleness and wisdom and placed him in the role of Friar Tuck. That's all right with Johnny. He is an agreeable young man.

The package with this letter arrives in your hand after a long contemplative discussion, not taken lightly. Sam and I (Johnny, too) are favorably impressed with the story you wrote us about Frances Elizabeth Quinn. Clearly, she is a bold and honorable woman, fighting for the cause of the Union. We are proud of the assistance you provided in protecting her.

We understand your sentiment on how your relationship with Frances, though loving and genuine, cannot develop into a lasting bond beyond friendship, but the emotion you express tells us that there well might come a time, even in war, when you feel the urge to commit your devotion to one special lady, and the diamond ring could be the perfect symbol with which to seal the pledge.

It is, of course, the engagement ring you gave your loving Mary years ago. We have kept it for you, together with her wedding band, ever since the day she was laid to rest. We will safeguard the band 'til your return, a battlefield wedding being unlikely. As a woman, I strongly sense that we should be giving you this ring as an opportunity for an expression of love, should you feel it one day. Your Mary would want it that way. Our love and prayers remain with you.

Affectionately,
Sydney Laughlin

I open the package. With memories of Mary flooding my emotions, I let the packaging drop and finger the ring. It seems so long ago I was placing it on her delicate hand.

I am entranced by those words, "Your Mary would want it that way." Sitting on my cot, I am frozen in time. I am overflowing with gratitude that my sister-in-law would be so very thoughtful. That Sam would be so supportive. Most of all, I know they have entered my very soul. To be sure, my life in the army is surrounded by women: women like Emma helping Grant, Jamie helping Frances, Frances helping the cause.

There are women near me to be pitied: those who scream from windows, the camp prostitutes, the Indian basket weavers. I am finding myself struggling that the Union's army should be a more perfect union, and that I might one day find in a woman somewhere, where we could forge a more perfect union for her and me.

The ring disappears into my fist. I rub my thumb over its facets and crown. Only God knows if there's another hand destined to wear it. The letter slips from my fingers and lands at my feet.

Chapter Eleven

With the conflict at Bolivar resolved, I'm back working the railroad tracks when the news arrives that Mortimer Leggett has been promoted to general! His former schoolboys look as if their old teacher has been promoted to principal. Before I can fully absorb this fantastic news, one of Leggett's emissaries gallops up along the railroad tracks with a riderless horse beside him. "Private Laughlin, I have orders to bring you to Gen. Leggett, sir. Immediately!"

Dread crawls down my spine in droplets. Is this the axe? What's the penalty for harboring a military criminal? I'm sweating, and not from working the tracks.

Mindlessly, I put down my hammer and mount the spare horse, a frisky filly. I'm led to the field headquarters under an overcast and brooding sky. Upon arrival, I dismount and wave to the orderly receiving the filly. Leggett's tent is wet from the morning rain. I walk gingerly to the entrance. The interior is illuminated by a single oil lamp above the commander's desk. I take my position just inside the door. My breathing is shallow, and sweat dampens my forehead as I wait for the verdict.

"Have a seat, son," he finally says, gesturing to a folding chair in front of him. I do as I'm told. My eyes temporarily refuse to focus, and the smoke wisping from the oil lamp nearly makes me sneeze. I strain to hold it back.

Leggett continues. "You watched Lt. Col. Hogg as he unselfishly devoted the last of his strength to the Union cause."

I force myself not to tremble. Is he going to hit me on valor? "I did indeed, sir."

"You understand that such devotion to military duty is the very lifeblood of this regiment's service, do you not?"

"With all my heart, sir."

"I've read the report about you and the lady impersonator. " He deposits his tobacco juice into a spittoon beside his desk and clears his throat.

This is it! I'm down the latrine. I'm going to get the book thrown at me.

"Is it true," he adds, "that you aided and sheltered her?"

"Well, you see..."

Leggett cuts me off, "Just yes or no!"

"Yes, sir."

He strokes his beard. "Interesting!" He leafs through a volume in front of him. "You're aware such behavior qualifies as harboring a fugitive?"

A swamp mosquito invades my ear, buzzing. I dare not swing at it. I blow at it instead, and Leggett narrows his gaze.

Leggett runs his finger through the document spread before him. "'The infraction thereof shall engender the consequence of up to two months confinement without pay.'"

I close my eyes and gulp. Where is he going?

Leggett licks his finger and turns the page. "There is a foot-note. 'The consequence of harboring a non-aggravated fugitive from justice shall be determined at the discretion of the commanding officer.'"

He closes the book and puts it down on his desk with a plop and stares at me. "Laughlin, your case exemplifies outstanding empathy toward a comrade in distress, and to a poor runaway as well. Your kind of humane commitment is a rare gem in this man's army. You were due for a promotion for your exemplary service with Wallace back at Shiloh. Today, you distinguished yourself once more against the forces of Van Dorn. You are both a soldier and a gentleman! I have put in orders for your promotion to the rank of second sergeant, with appropriate pay back-ordered to May 1st."

I was not prepared for this. My expectation was hearing a clink in the guardhouse. I blurt, "I don't know what to say, sir."

"Say you'll go back to work. Sherman has got to keep the tracks open, not only to advance toward Vicksburg, but also for shipping cotton up North to finance the war. And trouble is brewing at Iuka. We must move on. But take this warning with you: another appearance before me might bring different outcomes." He gives me a salute, "Dismissed!"

I return the formality, exit in military rigidity, and, for a moment, I stand in the rain outside, processing the incredulous impact of what just transpired. The panic of walking into his office now melts like flowing candle wax and hardens into a benign memory.

Before returning to the railroad tracks, I can't help but pass by George's tent to share the news.

"I'm happy for you," George says. "I drew the unsavory duty of recovering the dead, to prepare them for burial or transport.

"There are a lot of rifles been left on that battlefield that misfired. Guns that burst their muzzle with their tampion plugs in place. Some of them had been double-charged without noticing that the piece had not fired."

"Lacking training," I say, somewhat relieved that George

was occupying his mind with something other than women and dead bodies. "You know, George, we hardly got any sort of marksmanship training at Camp Gilbert. It's the same all over." Once again, imperfect human frailties are being put to overwhelming tasks.

"Yeah," says George, "and some of the guns had their stocks broken off, like it was done on purpose." He laughs and makes a gesture like snapping a twig.

"No," I answer. "It's done by men being taken prisoner, so the weapon can't be used by their captors." The notion occurs to me: The prisoners we take are just kids, barely eighteen, most of them.

I return to the railroad tracks and wonder what 'trouble' is brewing in Iuka? Men who've been there tell about its sulfur spring. I doubt if we're heading to some sort of vacation in a resort. I see us as an auxiliary force, but auxiliary to whom? And what kind of enemy? Not knowing the fight is almost as bad as the battle.

Chapter Twelve

"We're moving out to Iuka, gentlemen," Leggett announces. "William Rosencrans' Army of the Tennessee needs us. He's traveling to reinforce our garrison at Nashville, and that sneaky rascal Sterling Price got wind of it. We will accompany Gen. Edward O. C. Ord's division to head off Price's advance. Ord should be arriving before us."

We march into a blustering, windy night. No moonlit sky this time. If Sterling Price is a "sneaky rascal," what kind of stealth must we watch for? I take some comfort knowing Ord's army is meant to be in place before we arrive. We've heard of his reputation, his role in opening California during the gold rush, and his friendship with Sherman from West Point.

Sure enough, men bathe in hot sulfur springs. Grant has instructed us not to engage until we know of Rosencrans' arrival by "the noise of battle." So, we stack arms and settle in with Charles Ruper's sweet "Tatoo" bugle call, summoning us to rest.

Secure the perimeter. Ready for sleep. Non-essential fires and talk to cease in 15 minutes.

Morning brings coffee and crackers. Ord decides he needs an eye on the enemy, so he takes a band of us to recon. The only road to their works is heavily protected with artillery, and the alternative is to trudge through the swamp. Roots, weeds, slime, and water moccasins meet our brigade as we lead out front.

We are surprised to find Price's Confederate camp entirely deserted, as abandoned as the resorts, their "Accommodations" signs dangling helplessly over their oaken doors.

What happened? Where is Rosencrans?

"I saw a newspaper office on Bank Street," says George. "News reporters should know. 'The power of the press,' you always say!"

"Brilliant, George!"

We find a short, red-haired man in the *Times* office. He looks up from cleaning his press when we enter. "Your Rosencrans did arrive early in the morning. He must have been brave or foolish, taking on Sterling Price without reinforcements!"

Rosencrans was here, and we were of no help?

"That was supposed to be us," I confess, "with Edward Ord's army. We had orders from Grant to wait 'til the noise of battle began. Not a single one of us heard it!" I shudder. Men might have died because we were not there!

"That is strange," says the newsman. "But there was indeed a lot of wind. It can carry sounds away, and you don't hear it. Your Rosencrans came running into my office. I let him use my telegraph to call Grant for reinforcements, but the line had been cut. Rosencrans sent a messenger, but Sterling Price broke through Rosencrans's line. Lots of men were killed. I know how y'all must feel."

We thank him for his information. The tragedy brings back

the memory of my not being present for Mary, and I try to shake it away.

"Have you any information, sir, about Sterling Price? How did he know of Rosencrans' march toward Nashville?"

"Sterling Price is sly like a fox!" He continues, "And he knows how to evade capture. He's got one of the smartest-ass bushwhackers running with him, he does."

I don't need a tale-telling. "Where is Rosencrans?"

The newsman grabs a rag and wipes the grease off his hands. "You gentlemen want to see him?"

"Of course!"

"He's right over by the depot. Got a whole raft of reporters gathered 'round."

"Thanks," we scramble out, not taking the time to close the door behind us.

"Hey!" the man shouts after us. "Shut the door, the wind's scattering my papers!"

We don't stop. We hurry toward the depot, trying to balance our guilt against the explanation of wind and silence. Could it really be that simple?

We reach the back of the crowd, jostling and shivering. Flags wave overhead. We stretch for a view. Rosencrans stands at the center. He answers questions freely, unlike most commanders. The men love him for it.

He does not spare Grant, openly criticizing his vague orders and blaming us for failure to hear the noise of battle.

Gasps ripple through the crowd. Though the boys admire "Rosy," my stomach knots. Officers are squabbling in public, and blame is being slung like mud, all while men bleed.

By noon, the telegraph is working again, and we're ordered to return to Corinth. Leggett tells us that after Iuka, Sterling Price joined forces with our old enemy, Earl Van Dorn, in an attempt to retake Corinth.

By morning, Corinth is reinforced with two divisions of Ord's army, fresh rations, and ammunition. The position holds. Our 78th is ordered to continue its march toward Nashville. Price is blocked.

As I turn Rosencrans' accomplishment over in my mind, the newsman's earlier remark about Price's bushwhacker resurfaces.

"Yes," he'd said, tapping his press. "Howard 'Doc' Rayburn. Just a kid, but notorious. Stole a Yankee officer's horse right from under his nose. Disguised himself as a woman, danced with the officer, coaxed him into braggin' about his fine black stallion. By nightfall it was gone."

I admire Rosencrans' fire, his refusal to bend, despite my guilt over not being there when he needed us.

Another long march through foul weather brings us to Nashville, only to find Bragg's army already in full retreat. We pivot to keep the rebels from returning.

Leaving Nashville, we pass a team of Union doctors heading in.

"Are there wounded still inside the city?" we ask.

"Yes," one replies. "Hospitals are overflowing, both military and civilian. But that's not why we're here." He removes his spectacles and looks us squarely in the eye. "We're here to examine the local working girls. The brass says venereal disease is thinning the ranks. Shipping the women downriver didn't work, so Col. Spalding and Gen. Granger devised a mandatory licensure program."

The words sit wrong with me. "Times are hard for those women," I say. "I suspect they'd rather do anything else, but there's no work."

"The military's eaten the town alive," he answers. "Supplies are scarce. Jobs are gone. Some of those girls were schoolchildren not long ago. We can't have our boys carrying syphilis and gonorrhea home."

I glance at George. "Did you?"

"Definitely not," he says, firm. "You warned me, William."

The doctor's mention of schoolgirls burns my eyes. I hold it in and move on. "Any news from Corinth?"

"Rosencrans arrived in time. Rebels woke up surrounded. Artillery tore holes in their line. It went all the way down to hand-to-hand. Men fell so fast they had to watch their footing. Van Dorn punched through twice, but Rosencrans rode to the front shouting, 'Soldiers! Stand by our country!' Bullets knocked his hat clean off, but his men surged forward and reclaimed the batteries. Van Dorn retreated."

Gratitude swells in my chest. The man we failed to protect pulled through anyway.

"For that loss," the doctor adds, "Robert E. Lee replaced Van Dorn with John C. Pemberton."

Chapter Thirteen

The rolling countryside is scarred with columns of smoke rising from rebel villages that once dotted the land. We're out of Nashville, moving down dusty roads back toward Bolivar. The destruction of both the Federal and Confederate forces tightens my throat. George still doesn't see the point of it all. It's hard enough for me to face it. At some point, a man has to ask, how much devastation is enough?

As we pass burned-out plantations, black families wave and call out, "That's right!" and "Good for you!" They no longer believe we have horns and cloven feet, as they were once told, and many fall behind us, walking in our tracks. Most have no shoes. They accept the wreckage and move on.

On rocky trails, we pass fences fully ablaze. Women, ragged and soot-smeared, tear down rails to stop the fire's spread. Their enslaved workers have fled. Without menfolk, they scramble to haul out what they can, a grand piano, its lacquer blistered and blackened. Their husbands, they tell us, have gone off to "pursue their rights." Whether they know it or not, those "rights" to own people will end on January 1st. It's November now. They're caught in a fate they didn't choose.

As grim as it is to watch in the falling dusk, we fall back on the logic that we're not responsible for guarding their homes, or their piano, while their men rain fire and lead on us elsewhere. Each man is sorting his own morality these days. I wonder how the women in my family would face this. How is my gentle sister Margaret's back? Does practical Mary still battle migraines? And steadfast Sydney, raising my son.

The fence rails the women pulled down become our firewood the next night. They burn hot and clean. Our camps stretch in a line of flames. Downwind, the Confederate cavalry hidden nearby is smoked out and rushes us near Davis Mill. It's more drilling than battle. After half an hour of skirmishing, they gallop off.

Our brigade, now under Gen. Leggett, has received 800 new recruits. Rations, however, have not followed. My wagons are empty. Foraging brings in what it can, including slaughtered hogs. I can't help thinking of Castleberry's pig, Bowser. No time for that now. We're called to assembly to hear a dispatch from our old commander, Henry Halleck, writing from the War Department.

The budget is cramped. Is he telling us? Large tents are to be replaced by small ones, carried on the soldiers' backs. Transport is cut to four wagons. I ache at the thought of leaving animals I trained for so long. War presents hard choices.

A correspondent from the *Chicago Tribune* travels with us, writing about the effect of the cuts. I could tell him plenty. It isn't just hunger or weight. It's not knowing how long this will last. Months? Years? Lives? Uncertainty wears a man down faster than marching.

The paymaster is late again. If we want soap or a newspaper, we use sutler tokens, worthless except at inflated prices.

The boys trade those chips among themselves at fair value. Too bad morality can't be exchanged the same way, trading great wrongs for lesser ones.

LaGrange, Mississippi
November 9, 1862

My Dear Sisters,

I steal this quiet moment. By the time this reaches you, Christmas will have passed, and I'll be somewhere with my wagons and my Springfield musket. I imagine Ohio is far colder than Mississippi.

The hardest part of this war is resisting the guilt that comes with maiming and killing other Americans. Sometimes men miss on purpose when they can see an enemy's face. I could not, when a massive rebel came at me. If I hadn't taken part of his arm, I wouldn't be writing now.

Another strain is the childlike rivalry among some officers. A dispute followed Iuka between Grant and Rosencrans. I expect men in command to settle differences and press on, but perhaps I'd feel differently under that burden.

The bugle is sounding. Give my love to the family. Mary, thank your husband Jacob for teaching me persistence. Margaret, your letters and

*spirit mean more than you know. Thank Sam and
Sydney for the loving care they give Johnny.
Your loyal brother,
William*

As I seal the letter, the thoughts keep coming. Writing steadies me, confusion thins to a line I can follow. The drawback is time and inkwells that leak into your gear.

At the mail office, a group of Southern gentlemen and a Confederate major are escorted in for questioning. The assistant adjutant general addresses him.

"I believe we've met before, Major."

"Yes, sir."

"You were among those captured at Fort Donelson. I put you on a train to Chicago."

"You did."

"How did you return to the ranks?"

"I'm not required to say."

"You're shielded by the flag you rebel against," the adjutant snaps. "You'll join others of your kind in Alton, Illinois." Then to the guards, " Take him."

I'm not the only one writing letters here. Camp talk buzzes about a note Grant sent Halleck about a pair of ladies' undergarments.

*To Maj. Gen. Henry W. Halleck
LaGrange, Mississippi
November 26, 1862*

*General Halleck,
Having come across a pair of unmentionables in*

a deserted rebel house, I naturally wondered who might benefit from them. I can think of no one but Col. Thom of your staff. They are therefore respectfully donated to him, with such remarks as you choose to make.

Very respectfully,
Your Obt. Svt.,
U. S. Grant

Is this payback to Halleck for easing him out of field command after Shiloh? Whatever Grant's motive, the note belittles women! The underwear might have been planted in the house to insult Grant.

"Even if the woman was a rebel," I say to the men, "the joke shows disrespect. What will Julia think when this reaches the papers? Only a man unsure of himself pulls a stunt like that."

We sit around the fire with Ted Szewzyski, Marshal Yetman, George, and two Missouri boys, Elmer Burdette and Josh Cardiff. December bites the air.

"You can't always judge Southern girls," Burdette says. "That underwear might've been left as a trophy."

"How are they different from Yankee girls?" I ask.

"Josh and I went out foraging and found this large chicken coop. A group of Indians was there foraging for pigs in the nearby pasture. The farmwoman, she comes running out of the house and yells at us."

Szewzyski leans forward, eyes wide. "And not at the Indians. Is that the difference?"

"No," he says, spitting a plug of tobacco into the fire. "She's telling us that we may take the chickens, but won't we please stay until the Indians have left. We told her the Indians only want some hogs, and we will return after delivering the chickens to camp. As we left, the Indians ran straight into a bushwhacker camp, and the shooting started. Outgunned, the bushwhackers took off, leaving a wagon. Back at the campsite, a sutler was looking for his wagon, so he rode with us on the return to the farm."

"Were items missing?" asks George.

"Some of his merchandise was missing, but the woman said she didn't know anything about them. We checked the house. All of the missing items were under her floorboards!"

"Are you saying," Yetman proposes, "that Northern girls are never deceitful?"

"Not never," says Burdette. "But there are a lot of ladies in the South, you know, pulling tricks."

"That Southern farmwoman was desperate," I insist.

"No different from any other." I can imagine my sister Mary Glessner doing the same under stressful conditions! But I am more concerned for the woman's safety than for comparisons. I grab a stick nearby and stir up the embers now waning in the fire, pondering an alternative to the self-serving perspective.

"Wouldn't it have been wise to leave a guard with her? You rode off and left her with a bunch of Indians after she was kind enough to give you her chickens."

Burdette glances at Josh. "Never thought of it that way."

Chapter Fourteen

Later in the month, my friend Marshal Yetman is beside himself. Ulysses Grant, in charge of selling the confiscated cotton to merchants who ship it northward, issues the permits to merchants who buy the cotton. Black market buyers, without permits, bribe U.S. officers to sell it to them, and Grant blames the Jews for the breach of regulations. Marshal's dad is one of the merchants being targeted.

Marshal Yetman, Levi Gould, and Israel Fisher are distraught over General Grant's General Order No. 11, issued December 17th. It calls for all Jews to be expelled from the department within twenty-four hours, regardless of conduct. My friends know respectable Jewish families here. Some welcomed them for Sabbath meals, and none of them had any part in the black market.

Letters and telegrams have begun flooding the War Department in Washington, objecting to Grant's order. Marshal's dad appeals directly to President Lincoln. Soon, we're told Lincoln directed Halleck to instruct Grant to revoke his order. When will our otherwise brilliant field commanders stop making bad decisions?

The commanders compound their errors at our supply depot in Holly Springs. Near the Tallahatchie River, we hear cannon booming from Col. Robert Murphy's fortifications two miles out on December 21st. Too late. Earl Van Dorn has slipped in at dawn and raided the fully loaded depot. 15,000 dollars' worth of supplies are gone.

The few hundred men defending the garrison were captured before we arrived, and now they're standing here talking to us.

"You're still here?"

"Battered, but alive."

"Did you escape Van Dorn?"

"No. He had us lay down our arms and paroled us."

"So which way did he go?"

"North, from what we heard, wrecking bridges and rail lines to foul your advance. They left in a hurry, like they'd gotten urgent news."

The sound we heard wasn't only a cannon. Van Dorn set the torch to the powder magazine. Windows across town lay shattered. Wells are ruined. Women, children, and old men haul water from the river two miles off.

"Is this kind of deprivation really necessary?" I ask Jose Fleisher. "Especially laid on women?"

"You should hear how those fancy ladies treat us," Jose snaps. "Look there, see them strutting in their Sunday best? Pass under their windows, and they'll spit insults through the broken glass."

"I've noticed," I say, watching a frail woman and an elderly man stagger past with water pails. "And I think I know why. Southern men treat women as property. The women own nothing but their slaves, and now the slaves are walking. Fine dresses or not, they're at the bottom. And we're the ones forcing the change."

"Simon and Hal can show you how to fix that," Fleisher says, ignoring me. "See that house across the street, the shutters closed tight?"

"I see it," I say, already uneasy.

"Well, yesterday, the women inside screamed filth at them. Simon and Hal went back at ten that night, knocked, and entered. As the daughters bolted down the stairs and out back, the men told the old fellow they were there to teach him to discipline his girls."

"How?" I ask.

"They tossed him a rifle. Ran him through the Manual of Arms. Had him march for half an hour. Told him they'd be back the next night unless the insults stopped."

"Did it work?"

"When they came back, the shutters were closed."

"Did it teach respect or fear?" I ask.

No one answers. I imagine the question settling into them slowly. What if one of those women had fallen on the stairs? What did this prove, other than our power to frighten? What is a soldier's real responsibility?

This is the second time I've challenged my comrades over women. Who am I to judge? I feel pulled between being a hard soldier and a moral man, and not sure how to hold both.

Grant seems far less troubled. After the loss at Holly Springs, he decides Jackson must be taken before Vicksburg. Instead, we're ordered to march to Oxford. No one understands the detour.

Whatever his plan, Grant sweetens it. After breakfast, he announces that the first regiment to reach Oxford will receive advanced pay. How he managed that with the paymaster is anyone's guess.

We march in the mud. In the rain. In the snow. Wind bites our ears; fingers go numb. The dull thump-swish-thump of boots is joined by another sound. Those who dare break cadence glance back and see it, a long column of contraband people: men, women, children, babies bundled tight, all marching behind us.

A few of us manage to speak.

"Where you folks from?"

"Holly Springs, LaGrange, everywhere," a man says. "Y'all free, so we free." His smile falters. "Today's a special day, y'know."

"January first," someone says. "Emancipation."

"No, suh." He draws a finger across his throat. "Massuhs can still kill us. That paper doesn't stop 'em."

"So, what makes today special?"

"January first is when they sell off whoever they can to pay debts. Wife, chillun, don't matter. We call it Heartbreak Day."

Nothing has shown me so clearly what we're fighting for. Men wipe their eyes and pretend not to. These people have lost family, ripped away, a cruelty sharper than my own loss of Mary and little Marylee.

"Well," our boys say softly, "welcome to freedom."

Chapter Fifteen

"Up the road yonder, a little to the left, they's a schoolhouse," declares one of the negro men marching with us. "I know the schoolmaster there. He'll let y'all camp on the open playground 'n get rested up. And he'll have water, too!"

Heaven sent!

Gen. "Blackjack" Logan, marching with us, takes up the man's lead. "There's a house on the property," he says. "Would the schoolmaster allow us to use it as a field hospital? We've got wounded."

"Yes, suh, absolutely!" the man answers, grinning, pounding his fist into his palm. "Ol' Matthew'll say yes, and he'll fetch water from the well."

As we approach, children are crying, thin, tired sounds. They're hungry. "Only one meal a day," the schoolmaster says quietly. "We've had very little."

"Well, here." We pass out army crackers. The children hold them like jewels. Some nibble, careful and slow. Others devour theirs in seconds and lick the crumbs from their palms. Even the schoolmaster and the contraband families smile as they chew. I thank God Johnny eats every day back home.

The house is small but warm, with a wood stove breathing heat. A ragged mutt sleeps on the hearth. Atlases and reference books crowd a narrow shelf. An alphabet chart for cursive hangs crooked on the wall.

The wounded are carried inside. A padded drop-leaf table becomes an examination board. Treated men line the edges of the classroom, boots muddy, faces gray. When we move on, we leave the schoolmaster a chunk of salt pork. The sick and injured are sent on toward the nearest rail depot.

Hours later, we march for Oxford. We are tired, steadied, and a little proud of what we managed for those children. And our 78th win Grant's prize of advanced pay. "Lincoln was right," Grant says. "You can count on Ohio boys."

We pass through Oxford, Davis Mills, LaGrange, Moscow, Lafayette, not toward Vicksburg now, but Memphis. Fifteen miles out, we catch the train, not because we're fast, but because it's off the rails at Germantown. We see the wreck from the bend in the road.

Gen. Logan rides up to the engineer, who steps down from the cab.

"Everyone all right?"

"No, sir. Some are dead, I don't know how many, and about seventy-five are injured."

Logan strokes his black mustache. "Not surprising, with the way the rebels tear up tracks." He leans closer, sniffs. "You regulation? I smell liquor."

"Only a tad," the engineer pleads.

"Company C, help the medics!" Logan orders. "We move these patients to Memphis as soon as the rails are fixed."

The engineer spreads his hands. "Forrest's cavalry raids trains. I won't risk it with this many wounded."

Logan's voice hardens. "Company E, guard this locomotive!" He lifts his saber. "If this man moves the train without the sick, injured, and dead aboard, you are ordered to fire."

The engineer doesn't argue. Company E rides to Memphis, eyes split between the tree line and the reluctant man at the throttle.

We march on and stop at a speck called Abbeyville. A black family invites us to a belated Christmas in their shack. The woman insists on playing holiday tunes on her fiddle. They share a jug of homemade cider. They have almost nothing, yet give everything. I'm overwhelmed by it.

We cross the Tallahatchie in snow and freezing rain. We get lost. Logan steers us to an abandoned cotton gin. We don't stack arms, we jam them into frozen mud and collapse inside. Logan curses us soundly come morning. We shake it off. Memphis waits. He must feel it, too.

Memphis looks like a Northern city. Seven months after its capture, eight rebel vessels have been adapted. A baker selling doughnuts explains it. "During the naval fight," he says, wiping his hands, "our ships went down one by one."

"We've heard," Ted Szewzyski says, spreading his arms. "Lit the sky like Judgment Day."

"What folks remember," the baker says, "is your compassion. When our ship, the *Lovell*, went under, sailors from your flagship jumped into the water and pulled our men out. You don't see that often in war."

The words settle heavily. So much of this war lacks mercy. We thank him and stroll past prosperous houses. The women here are different, gracious, open, offering food and cold drinks. Lemonade. Sassafras.

For many men, the drink isn't sassafras. Whiskey's become a problem. New rules clamp down. Passes required. Two-at-a-time. Two hours only. I go with George to keep him straight, and myself, too.

That afternoon, we're at the Tugboat Tavern on Beale Street, George, Jose Fleisher, Ted Szewzyski, and me, cold beer sweating in our mugs. We talk about food, the miracle of fresh meals.

"Don't look for chow on Vance Avenue," Fleisher warns. "Hardcore seceshes."

"And avoid the women there," I add. "They'll charm every dollar from you."

George arches a brow. "And how would you know that, Will?"

"Relax," I say. "I ask the locals." Those women deserve pity more than scorn; they didn't choose that trade.

"Hey, Hall," Ted shouts, "how come you never had a woman?"

George fires back, "'Cause I'm almost as ugly as you, Szewzyski."

Laughter rolls.

"Easy," I say. "George is twenty. We don't need him desperate or out of regulation."

"Like you, Will?" Ted jabs.

I look away. Leggett might not be so generous another time.

Chapter Sixteen

s I turn toward the door, my eye catches a young woman entering the tavern. She takes a seat beside a gentleman at the bar, speaks with him briefly, and orders a drink. She wears a stiff white collar, a blue jacket, and a sailor's hat, the uniform of a Union Navy nurse. After a few minutes, the man rises, limping noticeably, and makes his way out.

Reading her as a woman of good character, I turn back to my companions. "Do you see the nurse at the bar? Let's stay a bit longer. Order another round. I'm going to invite her over, and you gentlemen will be on your very best behavior. Agreed?"

"Agreed," they chorus, half amused.

I cross the room, introduce myself, and ask if she will join us. She smiles and carries her drink to our table. George stands at once and offers his chair.

"Did you notice the gentleman I was speaking with?" she asks.

"Yes," all three say at once, though I know they hadn't.

"He was one of my first patients," she continues. "I'd just

joined the U.S. Nurses Corps. I was a freshman from Brimfield, Illinois, assigned to the steamship *John J. Roe* at Pittsburgh Landing. My husband, Jake Sinnott, had died of battle wounds. I told myself that if I could save even one man for the nation, then Jake would not have died in vain."

"My condolences, Mrs. Sinnott," I say softly.

She nods and goes on. "On my first day aboard the *Roe*, I heard a man crying from one of the cots. A sailor, his leg shattered just above the ankle by a cannon shot. When I unwrapped the bandage, I saw the problem at once. His ankle was out of joint.

"A surgeon passed by, and I told him so.

"'I guess it is not,' he snapped. I insisted. He smiled, demeaning, and said he'd call the ward surgeon.

"A dapper little man hurried over and barked, 'Where's the damned fool who says this man's ankle's out of joint?'

"'She's standing here,'" the first surgeon said.

"'It is not out of joint!' he declared.

"I stood my ground. He squatted, unwound the bandage in a rush, and began examining the joint. His hands slowed. Finally, he looked up and said, 'I take it all back. I beg your pardon. It is out of joint. I was too hurried to notice.'"

She smiles faintly at the memory. "He asked if I would help him set it. He held the leg. I pulled the foot. It went in with a snap. The sailor fell asleep at once, the first rest he'd had since the injury. He's the man you saw at the bar."

"That's a remarkable story, ma'am," I say.

"Eleanor," she corrects gently.

"Well then, Eleanor, we're impressed. Standing your ground like that, especially so new to service. It ought to be the standard in this war. What brings you to Memphis?"

"I'm receiving instruction across the street," she says, "on Dr. Thomas Holmes's new embalming process. We're learning how to prepare the fallen so they can be sent home cleanly, without decay.

"I've heard of it," I say. "But I've seen bodies badly damaged, limbs gone, bodies torn apart. Does it work then?"

"Not well," she admits. "The fluid must circulate through intact arteries. When the body is too damaged, burial is the only safe course. The worst cases are explosions, when there is nothing left to recover."

"I hope none of the men I respect ever meet such an end," I say.

My friends are so taken with Eleanor, her calm strength, her clear eyes, that they forget to order the last round. We thank her for her service and rise to go; our two hours are nearly up.

Those last minutes make the whole afternoon shine. What a woman, steady, compassionate, unbowed.

Roll call is held fifteen times a day now. It curbs drunkenness, mostly. Still, after the final call, women wander into camp selling pies, and sometimes whiskey, or, more sadly, themselves.

On February 20th, we move out again, bound for the boats. Vicksburg, perhaps, but no one says. A commander laughs, "If we don't lose our bean dippers before we get there, we'll do fine!" The ships lie at the dock for the Sabbath, and some men slip past the guards to spree through the city.

325 miles later, we camp on the Louisiana side of the river at Lake Providence, half a mile from the Mississippi. Fifty black laborers are cutting a canal between the lake and the river. Grant hopes to sail our boats through, severing the rebels' beef supply from Texas and slipping on to Vicksburg.

We're with Gen. "Black Jack" Logan again: our badges change so often our jackets look like pincushions. Our work is to carve the riverbanks and flood the bayou. We begin, then are abruptly ordered to Eagle Point, where Confederates threaten our gunboats. Up and out again.

We haven't gone far when the call comes back. Torrents from the Mississippi are rushing into Providence. The rebels have cut the levee.

People are drowning, clinging to horses, furniture, anything that floats. We run.

"Those who can swim, bring them to higher ground!" I shout. "Those who can't, stand ready to pull them out!"

I surprise myself. A second sergeant isn't meant to command like that, but the men move. Mothers clutch children. Horses plunge. Debris and insects churn in the brown water.

A family of twelve has found a loose door: two men, two women, and eight children. Some ride atop it; others cling to the edges.

I swim to the nearest man. "Take off your belt! Buckle it to the doorknob! Link the rest! Hand me the end!"

They work fast. I strike out toward shore, toeing the line. The current strengthens. My arms burn. Am I going under with them?

Then, the pull eases. A strong black arm is beside mine.

"We came to help," the man says.

"From where?" I gasp.

"From the canal upriver, suh. Brought a dozen of us."

"Much obliged. Your name?"

"Ebenezer, suh. From New Orleans."

"I'll see your valor acknowledged," I promise.

We dig two long trenches and guide the flood between them. At last, the water obeys.

I wonder if I'll ever be able to repay Ebenezer and his men.

By March 28th, we're camped fifteen miles downriver at Vista Plantation. Abandoned stores yield spirits, potatoes, dried fish, and brand-new drawers. Clean underwear feels like a miracle after swamping mud and gallinippers.

Ruper's bugle cuts through the air. Mail call. Everybody waits patiently to hear if his name is called. When I hear mine, fear rushes over me. If it's another announcement of someone's demise, I'm not sure I'll be able to take it.

Chapter Seventeen

Murfreesboro, Tennessee
December 30, 1862

My dear Sergeant Laughlin,
My heart still fills with gratitude every time
I think about the kind way you protected me back
at Corinth. You saved my life!
As I told you I would when I boarded the
train, I made it my business to continue in
defense of the nation. I created a new male iden-
tity and managed to enlist in Gen. William
Rosencrans's new Army of the Cumberland.
My build and strength fooled them. Before
long, I was made a wagoner, slower than you,
but still a surprise. I should have watched you
more closely. I had to rely on a farrier, and the
fewer eyes nearby, the safer I feel. When both

front wheels lost their tires, I couldn't manage the forge and had to ask a wheelwright. When he returned them, I reversed the threading on the hubs. Within minutes, the wheels came off.

They removed me from wagon duty. I became an orderly for Gen. Philip Sheridan. He tells me, "You have such blue eyes, you should've been born a girl." Little does he know.

We're scheduled to march out of Nashville tomorrow morning, New Year's Eve, in the bitter cold.

I hope this letter finds you well. I confess, I truly felt I was falling in love when you cared for me in your wagon. But I know it's impossible to cultivate a full loving relationship, as I am committed to maintaining this ruse and continuing in the service of our flag as long as I can. Stay well, dear William. Did you ever find out what became of that snake that was knocking on the sideboard of the wagon where I was hiding? And have you had any more close calls with that beast, Cyrus Braddox? You are twice the man as either of them.

And, by the way, determined to stay clean as well as to serve, I have found a sneaky way to bathe without being seen!

Fondly,

Richard Glessner

Frances Elizabeth Quinn

H eaven blesses you, Fanny-Liz! Rosencrans' leadership so fits her personality. She is a survivor, as he is. I revel in the purity of her character and her valor.

Frances is right. Much as a lasting relationship with her would delight me beyond words, her star is in a different quadrant than mine. But I will always be inspired by her resilience.

Historical images

#1. The Laughlin brothers: (l to r) Samuel, Alexander, William

#4. Tooled leather wallet of George C. Hall

#5. Confederate pewter belt buckle

#6. Brass cargo or luggage tag

The night's getting late and soon we must part,
Pray tell me have I an interest yet in your heart.

#7. Love note clipping

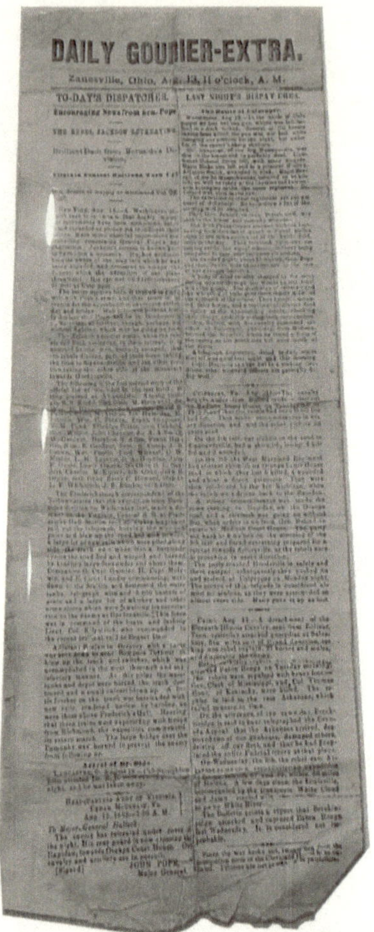

#8. *Zanesville Courier (misspelled) reporting Battle of Culpepper*

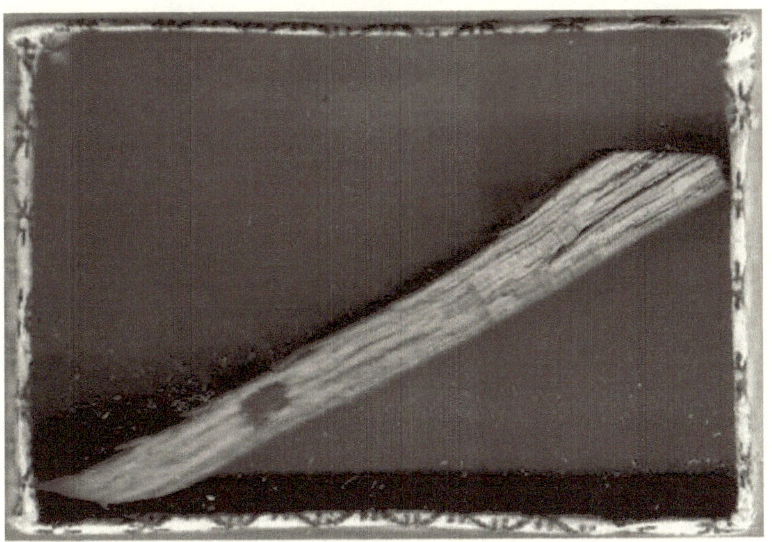

*#10. Wood fragment from oak tree where Pemberton surrendered
Vicksburg*

Chapter Eighteen

Our bedding is gone. Stolen, we figure, by another regiment as a joke. With nothing to lie on but the soggy forest floor, we help ourselves to the boards and shingles from an old cotton gin. The next morning, as we leave the "crime scene," smoke curls into the air. Something in the structure has caught fire, and the scent of smoldering wood follows us back to camp.

When our shenanigans get reported to Gen. Logan, he sends an emissary to call us to his tent. "You gentlemen know full well that we are not to damage civilian property unless we are under orders to do so. A soldier who takes it upon himself to steal or destroy property causes discord in the ranks that cannot be tolerated.

"Now you will go right back and recoup every board and shingle you took! You will each make your separate pile right here." He points with his sword. "My orderlies will carefully tabulate the damage for my report of your waywardness."

We do as we are told and wait in silence while his orderles

itemize all our piles and read their reports. At last, Logan says again, "Sergeant Laughlin, today's date!"

"April first, sir."

"Indeed. April Fool's Day. You may now reclaim your boards and shingles."

The camp erupts with laughter, and men swapping old prank stories, but I cannot share in the mirth. Something gnaws at me. Ted whispers to me with a nudge.

"Did you see a hog run out of that gin?"

"No." I'm shaking now.

"Skull tattoo on his flank."

"Bowser!" I mutter. "The 124th Illinois...and Castleberry."

We make no accusations, but later Ted tells me Logan discovered a secesionist farmer had set the fire himself. "He wanted to roast us alive," Ted says, laughing it off.

But I can't shake the pit in my stomach. This wasn't just some April Fool's prank. Castleberry is intent on doing us harm, or at least wishing to keep us feeling damned edgy.

When will he strike next?

Two weeks pass with that question gnawing at me. On April 14th, orders came to advance toward Monroe, Louisiana. Before leaving Providence, Grant posts a garrison at Milliken's Bend to serve as both a supply depot and a training base for the United States Colored Troops, USCT. Former slaves are proving invaluable, both to the war effort and to themselves.

At Monroe, we are sent immediately to the General Hospital. The sight overwhelms us: walls packed with wounded Confederate soldiers. Overflow spills into schools, churches, hotels, and even a carriage shop. Sanitation is dire. We're asked to help move patients by rail to a new facility in Vienna. It is mournful work, but necessary. Among the wounded, partisan lines dissolve. We serve broken bodies, not causes.

Once the job is complete, we cross the Ouachita River, burn the bridge behind us, and take Camp Moore without resistance. It had been a Confederate training ground, where enslaved people were used not as soldiers but as laborers. We freed more than a thousand men and women captured by Confederate patrols while fleeing plantations.

Some choose to remain in Camp Moore as guards, being trained by negro operators from the 3rd U.S. Heavy Artillery. Others, still suffering from dog bites, choose to join the march. We protect them fiercely.

We march on and pitch camp, just in time to be hit by an unexpected nor'easter.

Tents rip free and scatter across the meadow. As we chase canvas through mud and rain, Sherman sits dry in his tent, evaluating his failed attempt to redirect the Mississippi. Rebels are filling our canals with felled timber faster than we can clear them. Once the chaos calms down, he makes two decisions.

Number one: to tell Grant the project is a failure and find a crossing back over the river in a different way, and number two, to tell the officer of the day to set up a muster.

On April 30th, the bugle sounds. We drop what we're doing and stand at attention on the drill fields. Gen. Sherman walks the line, inspecting us. One by one, the names are called to step forward.

"Pvt. Joseph Valkirk, step forward!

"Pvt. Philander S. Castor, step forward!

"Sgt. Andrew McDaniel, step forward!

"Lt. James Caldwell, step forward!"

Each promotion earns a shout of "Hi-Yo!" from the ranks.

Then my name is called. "For his devoted leadership in the river project, and for taking command of rescuing the citizens of Providence in the state of Louisiana, Sgt. William M. Laughlin is hereby promoted to the rank of First Sergeant."

The crowd yells, "Hi-Yo!" and bursts into applause.

I salute. "Permission to give credit, sir."

"Granted."

"To a black man who completed my rescue operation, sir. He brought men from the U.S. Canal Project upriver when he heard of the flooding of Providence."

"And what might be this gentleman's name?"

"Ebeneezer, sir."

"Inscription on the record needs a last name."

"He just referred to himself as Ebeneezer from New Orleans, sir."

He turns to his clerk. "The clerk will record: Distinction For Valor Beyond Call of Duty to Mr. Ebeneezer New Orleans."

The clerk complies.

Later, I write to my sisters and Sam and Syd. But in reality, aside from better pay, the rank promotion is not as important to me now as is my growing sense of purpose.

As far as crossing back over the Mississippi, Grant has made several attempts to do so against Vicksburg's defenses. When the attempt to cross at Grand Gulf fails, northern editorials begin asking for Grant's removal. Lincoln refuses to remove him, just repeats his familiar response, "I can't spare this man—he fights!"

Admiral David Porter successfully sails first his gunboats, and then his supply boats, past the rebel batteries on Vicksburg's shoreline by night. That is no small maneuver, due to the large north bend in the river, requiring slow speed with increased vulnerability.

Encouraged by Porter's maritime success, Grant moves us in Gen. McClernand's division farther southward, down from our swampy west side of the river, to seek an accessible crossing point. He and Sherman set up clever diversionary movements north and east of Vicksburg to distract the enemy.

Informed of a favorable crossing point by a local colored gentleman, we arrive at Bruinsburg. Without the colored folk, this war would be longer and bloodier!

There at Bruinsburg, we meet the U.S. flotilla, board, and cross the river accompanied by a military band playing "The Stars & Stripes Forever." Spearheaded by the leadership of Gen. McClernand under a clear moonlit sky, 17,000 men march across the east bank of the Mississippi toward Port Gibson. Definitely a march of triumph!

On the outskirts of Port Gibson, we meet a guard of rebels. We exchange fire, driving them back to Big Black River. Our march continues eastward on a road recommended by a negro couple. At midnight, we arrive near a farm occupied by a Mrs. Shaifer. Unfortunately for her, a Confederate general, Martin Green, is also at that farm, attending his picket line. He observes Mrs. Shaifer with some other women anxiously packing a wagon in fear of our advance.

He saunters up to the women and announces, "The Yankees will not be marching in the dead of night, I assure you, because of reduced vision." In this instance, he is wrong. Scarcely is a word out of his mouth before a shot bursts through the quiet night air. A dog barks.

Green's pickets open fire, and soon the air is alive with musket balls blasting from both sides. The horrified women scream and jump into their packed wagon, now drilled with bullet holes, and drive their horses full-speed out of the area.

Green hurries to a brigade posted near a church to arouse his men. More Union troops pour into the meadow. The woods around the Shaifer house rumble with artillery. The fight continues in fierce combat until 3:00 a.m. As the sun rises on the foggy morning, gunfire resumes with intensity.

McClernand moves his entire corps against Green's regiment. Reinforcements join him, both from CSA infantry and artillery. The men with our Gen. Peter Osterhaus begin shattering Green's line.

The Confederate commander brings in yet more reinforcements to Magnolia Church, but it is too late. We have him surrounded. Bowen orders a retreat, leaving his dead and wounded where they fell. The garrison at Port Gibson evacuates. It has been a stressful battle, made worse by Greene's chosen proximity to terrified women, but the Union now owns a foothold on Vicksburg's side of the river.

When the fighting is over, and prisoners have been processed, Gen. Grant collects Generals McPherson, Logan, and Osterhaus together and calls us to assemble. He commends us by saying, "Boys, you have done well today, but you will have more of the same tomorrow."

He then calls for a comment from Peter Osterhaus, who is from Rheinland Prussia and known for witty remarks in his native accent. Mounted on his horse, Osterhaus declares, "Vell, boys, I dell you vat it is. You do as vell tomorrow as you do today, und ve vip dem repels, undill day can't eat sauerkraut!"

A chance to whip the rebels, sauerkraut notwithstanding, has not arrived the next day, but comes soon enough. Grant is making his special plan to advance against Vicksburg by encircling the city on all sides. The part to be played by our 78th is to go with McPherson to root out the rebels from nearby Raymond.

Our adversary, Pemberton, has sent a force led by John Gregg to cut off our advance, and is on its way. McPherson proceeds cautiously; he doesn't know the strength of Gregg's fighting force. In the uncertainty of the speculation, he's called reinforcements.

It's a very hot day today, May 12th. The march is dusty and

dry. Our water is low. Men and animals are feeling the effects: first parched lips, then a haunting dizziness. Fourteen-Mile Creek comes into view. How fortunate!

We simply have to stop. As we enter the belt of timber lining the creek, we hear the tramping and rumble coming toward us just a short distance over a wooded hill. John Gregg's rebels have arrived. From the extent of the sound, our guess is that he's only prepared for a small conflict.

Now we engage in a volley of raining death! Shots smash off rocks, trees, splashing into the creek where men are drinking, a creek that is floating men away in scarlet swirls.

Our entire line draws back. Gen. Logan (McPherson's second in command) will have nothing to do with a retreat. He rides forward into the face of the enemy. The boys describe Logan's outcry as "the shriek of an eagle!" Every one of our men returns to his place. Gregg is caught off guard, but he's hitting hard. As the flight continues, he knows he is outnumbered and begins faltering.

Damn! He's attacking over the left flank! We rush in. Gregg slips away on the other flank and back where he came from. He pulled a decoy, and McPherson fell for it!

Fatigued, McPherson does not pursue. We enter the city and collapse at the tavern where a fine dinner awaits us. The women of the town serve us the fried chicken and lemonade they prepared for their "victorious" rebel men. It's not the spoils of battle we've won. It's the resilience and empathy of the women making the moment memorable.

Sitting over my lemonade and chicken, I look at my right hand. Scraped, but not wounded. I'm blessed that it's not floating down Fourteen-Mile Creek in shreds.

Chapter Nineteen

A minuscule figure stands in the road ahead of us. McPherson slows the pace and raises his hand. We halt. It's a boy, black and unarmed.

"The road is clear all the way to Jackson," he declares proudly.

McPherson turns to his orderly. "Give the boy a reward."

"A greenback?" the orderly suggests.

"No. That would put him in danger. Slaves aren't permitted to carry money." McPherson thinks a moment. "Give him a biscuit."

The orderly pulls one from his knapsack. The boy takes it, grins, waves, and vanishes into the trees.

The little scout was right. We march into Jackson without resistance. I think of Johnny—his age, his hunger to matter, and wonder what valor he may already carry inside him.

The echo of our boots replaces the battle we expected. Once proud to raise the Confederate banner, the capital yields without a shot. They hand over the courthouse keys.

Inside the conference room, we discover we've interrupted a citizens' meeting.

"We were trying to ferret out suspicious-looking persons," the chairman explains, "folks might be distributin' arms. We don't want any whippersnappers startin' a shootin' match."

George repeats the words later, nearly verbatim. I marvel at his memory.

We stand at attention as Lt. Roberts of Company E climbs the cupola, removes the Confederate flag, and replaces it with the Stars and Stripes. It snaps in the May breeze, visible across the city.

Women flood the streets; hair loose, skirts hitched. At the barbershop, while we're shorn and scraped, the barber explains.

"The cavalry lit out this mornin' the minute they saw y'all comin'. Left the fairgrounds in a panic."

"Because they felt defenseless?" I ask.

"That's it, Mister." He flicks his apron. "I was cuttin' hair out there. The women were with 'em. When the men bolted east, the girls ran straight back to town."

"They offered no resistance at all?"

"None." He spreads his hands. "They weren't fit to fight."

"Why not?"

"There was this tall, ragged stranger," he says, fingers lifted like feathers. "Looked half Indian. Came in last night on a crutch with only one leg. Sold 'em home-brewed whiskey."

A roar bursts out of me. "Halle-bloody-lujah!" Pasquathalu is alive and still at work. I see him again in my mind, slung across my shoulders at Shiloh.

Surgeon Reeves joins us at the fairgrounds, examining the last of the bottles. He sniffs, rolls it, and touches a drop to his tongue.

"Laced with the juice of a potent root," he says. "Locks the joints. By morning, they'd barely manage their boots, let alone a saber."

Gratitude swells in my chest. Pasquale's war continues.

We search the houses. Rebel officers have shed uniforms and blended into the crowd, leaving behind brass and weapons, the boys happily claim.

The Bowen House, five stories beside the Capitol, becomes Grant's headquarters. He frees the black staff and pays them wages. Loyalty rewarded. I'm not allowed inside, but the workers whisper of luxury. This kind of liberation is becoming familiar. It feels right.

The next day, bands march through Jackson playing Yankee tunes. Musicians who can fight, what an advantage. Someone finds a bakery. Fresh bread. We buy everything with Confederate script bearing Robert E. Lee's portrait and the words *Deo Vindice*.

God is our defender. I wonder what God they believe is defending them. They won't take Union dollars. Reason says soon their money won't buy a thing.

Mail call comes. George gets two letters. One from his mother: Stay out of trouble, and one from his sister: Don't forget to have fun.

I receive two as well. One holds Johnny's drawing, a fisherman, careful and intent. I fold it and tuck it close. Margaret writes with worry and pride, congratulating me on my promotion.

The second letter nearly knocks me off my feet.

Bowling Green, Kentucky
January 3, 1863

Dear Will,

I promised to write, and here I am.

With Sheridan's cavalry, we rode out of Nashville and were surprised at Stones River by William Hardee's division in a New Year's Eve attack. We ended up cornered in a section of cedar forest called Hell's Half Acre. There I got shot in the right shoulder. Many of our wounded were carried off the battlefield by the chaplain, John Whitehead, for medical care. In fact, he is writing this letter for me while I can't move my arm.

In the striped tent, they discovered, of course, that I am a woman. Col. Timothy O'Meara outprocessed me and asked for my "real name." I lied and said "Eliza Miller." I assure you, dear William, I will enlist again after I recover. I refused to return to my family, and I was sent here to Bowling Green. I will find another recruiting officer.

I'll always treasure your kindness at Corinth. As long as you can serve, I will. I'm glad you're staying ahead of that snake Castleberry and that ox Braddox. You're man enough to outlast them both.

Somehow, I sense that, though our stars are in different quadrants, a woman is waiting for you. That may surprise you.

Fondly,

Frances Elizabeth Quinn

If Frances can be so committed to keep on enlisting, even after a shoulder wound, even after gender humiliation, how can I offer anything less?

Word arrives from the outskirts of Jackson: Pemberton is struggling to hold the Big Black River crossings. Reinforcements can't reach him. Johnston orders evacuation and wires Richmond:

JACKSON INDEFENSIBLE. I AM TOO LATE.

No reply comes. Our men have cut the telegraph. Rail crews bend heated tracks around trees: Sherman's neckties. The smell of bonfires drifts through the valley. We uncover ammunition by the crate, hogsheads of sugar, artillery, Enfields —and in the rail yard, a train already burning. The ammunition cars erupt like hell itself.

In the midst of it all, I think of Ebeneezer, Frances, and now Robert Hanson, our postmaster. With the rails destroyed, he carries mail on foot—thirty miles through swamps and fields, by night, hiding by day.

No wonder the mail takes time.

Meanwhile, Pemberton runs hard for Vicksburg.

Chapter Twenty

The stench of sweat rises from our musky uniforms and sinks into the leaf-molded forest floor as we trudge down the narrow trail toward Sid Champion's farm. Across the way, Pemberton is struggling to reverse the direction of his supply train—on a bridge, no less. A wagoner's nightmare, not unlike the one I withstood at Shiloh. But this time it's the enemy's headache.

On a hilltop cornfield, a rebel lookout spots our approach and sends a warning down the line. Determined to preserve an escape route, Pemberton meets us with a counterattack.

Our troops meet an untold volume of minie balls and every imaginable artillery fire.

I stand on the hitch of my ordinance wagon, unloading wooden cartridge boxes to our infantry with George assisting me. A minie ball comes right through my Brogan and into my right foot. I wince and grab my foot, and as I do, I see a broad, grinning face: that lumbering hulk who tried to kill me at Shiloh, Cyrus Braddox! This time, his gait is more pronounced from the wound I gave him back then. He is not accompanied this time by the pair who carried him off the field at Shiloh. Instead, he's with three men armed with Enfield rifles and dressed in sloppy, worn clothing. Who are they? And what are they up to, running with Braddox?

He pauses to reload, so I turn and take aim to fire at him. But at that instant, his bugler calls retreat, and Braddox turns and vanishes, ambling off into his line. My own shot earns me nothing but a throbbing toe. Big Cyrus and his vow of revenge are still loose in this war.

At camp, I talk with my friend Ted Szewzyski. "Braddox nearly got me today! He was with three of the strangest-looking bunch, all shaggy and slovenly! They didn't look like soldiers. One looked like a midget! Who do you suppose they were?"

Ted squints, stroking his beard. "Could be Archie Clement. Him, Dave Pool, and Bill Hendricks—Missouri bushwhackers. Some of the worst. They run under Bloody Bill Anderson. Archie's barely five feet tall. They call him Little Arch. Some call him the Scalper."

"Well," I say, "that gives me, and all of us, reason to watch out, especially if that gang is hooked up with Braddox!"

Braddox's commander ordered retreat because Grant sent two stalwarts to take the lookout hill. The enemy scattered, first for shelter in Champion's farmhouse (Sid Champion happens to be on Pemberton's staff), and then, in complete confusion, in the direction toward Big Black River.

Acting on their confusion, McPherson moves us to the crossroads, cutting off the Jackson Road and Vicksburg.

Cornered, the rebels counterattack weakly. We hear they called for Gen. Loring to help—and he refused.

Later, Hovey surveys the hill. "Champion's Hill was no cornfield," he says. "It was a hill of death."

How long does an advantage last before hell opens again? Our hunger doesn't answer.

Our rations are gone. We chew slippery elm bark until Matilda Champion's hogs come tearing through camp. We seize them and feast. Never has the bugler's mess call sounded sweeter.

Soupy, soupy, soupy without a single bean:
Coffee, coffee, coffee without a drop of cream:
Porky, porky, porky without a strip of lean!

The pork from Champion's farm is all lean enough.

We drive the enemy toward Baker's Creek. They fall back again, fortifying the Big Black River Bridge, only twenty miles from Vicksburg.

My big toe throbs. Surgeon Reeves has patched it well enough for walking, and walking will be required in that swamp. I think of Frances Elizabeth's shoulder wound and bite back any complaint.

A hospital steward tells me what a real shoulder wound looks like. A shattered joint. Surgeons twist the humerus and take the whole arm with it.

The Big Black River flows like the Yazoo, draining toward Vicksburg. Pemberton posts a garrison to hold the bridge; then they're to burns it once Loring crosses. Loring crosses elsewhere. Confusion breeds disaster.

The garrison guards have swamp and open ground in front of them, and eighteen cannons, which they never had time to prepare.

We advance past abandoned, wandering horses, slosh through the swamp and into the open, shouting ourselves hoarse. "The Yanks are here!" The sound electrifies the blood.

A skirmish snaps into battle. Gen. Peter Osterhaus is wounded, and that is enough.

The rebels try to flee, igniting the bridge as they go, but we reach them first. We wade the bayou and smash into their left. Three brutal minutes. We are over the parapets.

Muskets hit the ground. Men run for the river and plunge in. Some drift away, lifeless. The bridge burns. Smoke chokes the air.

Then white flags rise, fifty of them, fixed to bayonets. Others hoist bales of cotton instead. We take a harvest of prisoners.

In the rifle pits, we find the dead. My breath catches. One of them is a woman, dressed in a Confederate uniform. Another Frances, on the other side. She gave her life for her cause.

The next day, Grant's engineers lay pontoon bridges. We cross and push toward Vicksburg.

Chapter Twenty-One

Each blast echoes through my ribs as cannon fire makes the ground swell under our feet. Smoke rolls over the river, thick with the stink of black powder and sweat. Ol' Bobby Lee's proud "nail-head holding the South together" rips wide open under our assault on the shrinking defenses of Vicksburg. Better yet, word spreads through the ranks that Lee has lost his palate for Beauregard's Louisiana jambalaya in favor of Pemberton, the Virginia blue crab, to command the CSA's Western Theater.

Good news comes as we press toward Vicksburg. Every newspaper announces the establishment of the Restored Government of Virginia. President Lincoln endorses the restoration. My ancestral home of Wheeling is now the capital of the 35th state, West Virginia.

As we progress with Sherman toward Vicksburg, we stop in the little town of Tiffin, Mississippi. The day is hot and dry. A farmer comes along with a barrel of cider on a wagon, selling it for five cents a glass. The Massachusetts boys are out of money, so Jim Haley devises a plan. While the others keep the farmer busy with idle chatter, Jim fetches a long auger from the tool cart. He crawls under the wagon, empties the horses' water pails, and drills through the floorboard into the cider barrel. The pails fill. When the farmer draws cider for the officers, the barrel is dry.

We go from comedy to a deadly challenge. Ulysses Grant, famous for his three-pronged advances, organizes forces around Vicksburg. Sherman will come from the north by a trail aptly named the Graveyard Road. McClernand will come from the south. We will come with McPherson from the east on Jackson Road. My veins throb with excitement. This master plan demands a master execution.

Battles up and down the line cost us dearly. Grant turns to a different tactic. Men dig tunnels under the fortifications around Vicksburg's perimeter to set explosives. Leggett is in charge. One major fort, the Stockade Redan, stands firm at the start of the Graveyard Road.

Sherman knows that to lead his troops down the Graveyard Road, the Stockade Redan must be blown. His men dig and detonate 2,200 pounds of black powder. The blast is so loud that our unit hears it miles away on Jackson Road. We wonder if it kills any Federals. It does, indirectly. A massive crater opens. Hand-to-hand fighting erupts over the gap, and we take casualties.

Daring to move closer, Gen. Leggett, whom Sherman appoints to tunnel blasting, has a mine dug under the citadel wall itself. When the charge ignites, the blast rises fifty feet, burying scores of rebel defenders and eight of ours, including black allies. Gen. Logan must be treated for burns and wounds.

This is getting dangerous. With rebel numbers dwindling, do we need to press this hard?

Fighting turns savage in the gap, wrestling guns, grabbing bayonets, tossing grenades, yanking hair and beards, slugging it out with fists. We lose over a hundred men in that single fight. When Sherman says, "War is hell," he knows what he's talking about.

Finally, Grant decides he can risk no more losses. Siege is the only option. Thank God! Our forces ring the city while Admiral Porter's gunboats hammer it from the river.

Supply bases matter: wagoners like me depend on them. Upriver, our base at Bovina needs defending. The 78th Ohio is sent away from Vicksburg, up the Yazoo to Bovina. Duty calls.

When shocking things happen, news travels fast. On a Sunday, we hear that Grant has issued an ultimatum back at the siege:

ALL WOMEN OUT OF THE CITY.

No one comes out.

By the following Sunday, the women plead to leave under a flag of truce. Grant says they had their chance and must take the consequences.

I can't square that. Squatting on a river dock at the Yazoo with Ted Szewzyski and Jose Fleisher, I ask, "Did you hear? Grant wouldn't let the women come out when they pleaded?"

"Why should he?" Jose says. "They had their chance."

"They aren't chess pieces," I say. "They're women."

"So?"

"So, they function differently from men. How could he know what some were dealing with? Menstrual flow. Childbirth. Weaning an infant. Or how their captors might treat them. Military men can make deals. It could've been the worst possible time."

"Then the others should've come out," Jose says, pitching a stone into the river.

Before it sinks, I say, "Women help other women in need."

"Will's right," Ted says. "Grant doesn't know how to deal with women. At Shiloh, I saw him stop at a farmhouse where a soldier was abusing a woman. Grant sprang from his saddle, wrenched the musket away, and cracked the man with the stock. Then he rode off instead of taking him into custody. The woman had to choose, abandon her home, or risk the man's recovering."

"Isn't that chivalrous?" Jose asks.

"No," Ted says. "It left her alone with the danger."

Jose lowers his chin to his fists. "I guess there's a lot I don't understand either."

Whose job is it to teach them?

Another morning brings word of a truce offer. The rebels ask for a ninety-minute cease-fire. Grant agrees. Yankees and Rebs drink coffee together and talk. Coffee is a treat for Confederates; New Orleans is closed, and they've been drinking acorns and sweet potatoes. Ours comes from Stephen Allen Benson, a free black man in Liberia.

A soldier from the 13th Illinois finds his father and brother inside the city. They want to be taken prisoner. No such luck. They vow to defect at the first chance.

As with the women, we don't know what's happening behind those walls. Some Confederates ask for Yankees' addresses to visit after the war. Others say they petitioned Pemberton to surrender, even threatening his life. He vows to hold out 'til "one live man."

Serving at Bovina, we miss it all. We chase Confederates up the Yazoo to Chickasaw Bayou and capture a band with their supplies. My wagon train is so long, I pray we don't have to reverse as we did at Shiloh.

Losses follow. Adjutant Henry Abbot is shot through the neck and suffers a fractured skull.

During that fight, I notice something strange. Three disheveled fighters without uniforms raid my wagon train. One is very short. We fire, and they flee. When I tell the boys, no one has seen Big Cyrus Braddox, though they agree it must've been Archie Clement's bushwhackers. We conclude Braddox is freelancing with them. No wonder he shows up everywhere. Where the devil is he now?

Ordered back toward Vicksburg, we're attacked by a full brigade, eight killed, 56 wounded. No sign of Little Arch or Big Cyrus. Jacob Beisaker of Company E loses a leg. We send him on a hospital ship for Memphis, praying he'll receive care like Nurse Eleanor Sinnott's. He dies aboard ship.

72 days in, we return to Vicksburg and recoil. The city is out of water, food, and medical supplies. People live in caves. Dead horses, half-eaten, are dumped into the river. Sanitation is gone. Disease runs rampant. The stench of death hangs over everything.

July 3rd arrives. Every Union gun is stocked with 150 rounds for an Independence Day salute if the rebels don't capitulate.

Before day's end, two Confederate officers appear under a flag of truce and ask to be led blindfolded to Grant. They request a commission to arrange surrender terms. Pemberton can hold out no longer. Finally.

One officer says, "Enough iron has been thrown into Vicksburg to stock a foundry and build monuments for all who've fallen."

Grant's answer follows. The garrison will be treated with courtesy due to the prisoners of war.

Men on both sides hold their breath. Some taste victory. Some dread prison. All hope the waiting is over.

Another messenger requests a personal meeting. Grant agrees. They will meet on July 4th at three o'cllock beneath a large oak atop a hill.

Everyone gathers. Coffee passes from hand to hand. At three sharp, Grant arrives, cigar in his mouth. They sit on a fallen log. Pemberton speaks first, arguing that he should be granted terms of surrender, as even a foreign power got in the Mexican-American war.

Grant draws him aside. They stand beneath the oak, voices lost to leaves. We wait an hour.

When Grant finally announces the terms, everyone snaps to attention.

"The rebels will surrender, and 38,000 will be paroled."

Cheers erupt on both sides. Men rush to cut slivers from the oak. I get one for my sister Margaret. By sundown, nothing remains of the tree.

Vicksburg's citizens vow not to celebrate the Fourth "'til hell freezes over."

Word reaches us that Lincoln, sleeping on a cot in the White House telegraph room, buys beer for the operators and raises a toast when the news arrives. I wish someone could've photographed that, but photography demands stillness, and who would set a tripod by the president's bed?

We march into the city behind Gen. John A. Logan, bandaged from the explosion. Gen. Leggett raises the flag over the courthouse. Federals and Confederates crowd the streets, laughing, trading keepsakes. A rebel named Comstock gives me his CSA belt buckle; he's lost so much weight, only an officer's suspenders work for him.

I give him Confederate script and a worn horseshoe for luck. He laughs.

George trades his razor for a CSA toothbrush. "Whiskey will sanitize it, right?"

Chapter Twenty-Two

Back home in Ohio, foulness is brewing over conscription. The newspapers are full of stories and editorials. Because the war is intensifying, President Lincoln has put into effect the "Conscription Act of 1863." Draft resisters in Holmes County gather in protest, some 900 strong, in the Loudonville house of a Swiss immigrant, Laurant Blanchard. They've equipped it like a fortification with tunnels, breastworks, bayonets, cannons, and food supplies. That's a lot of work just to make a point.

Governor David Todd forces the Federal government to send in troops from the 30th Ohio Infantry to disperse the crowd. Some eighty protesters are indicted. Blanchard is sentenced to six months of hard labor at the penitentiary in Columbus, but the charges are eventually dropped. Historians call it "The Holmes County Rebellion." Local folks have a better name, Fort Fizzle.

What do my younger brothers think of the draft? Alexander? Sam? If Sam is worried, it isn't in his and Syd's letters.

Ohio isn't the only state where emotions run high. "A rich man's war and a poor man's fight," they're calling it. If you have 300 dollars, you can buy an exemption. Even if you're drafted and don't have the money, you can find some poor unfortunate and pay him to take your place. Immigrant Irishmen anticipating citizenship are subject to the draft. They attack Africans who, not yet citizens, are deferred. This kind of chicanery stirs agitation and desertion among people caught in the web. In the midst of it, my sister Mary finds it necessary to write.

757 Chestnut St.
Zanesville, Ohio
March 17, 1863

Dear William,

We pray for your safety and wellbeing. The draft riots in Ohio present danger enough right here at home. You know my two sons; there's John, and there's William, named after you. As young men, there is the question of their being drafted, so I feel obliged to let you know what is shaping up in that regard.

William is, at this time, only fifteen years old. Unless he volunteers, he will not have to go, unless the war drags on beyond three more years. Heaven forbids! Can you imagine? Our brother Alexander convinced young William to join him in taking over the Ohio City Nail Works in Wheeling! They are producing railroad tracks, so it looks like our brother Alex will be deferred.

John's is a different story. He is nearly twenty years old and has taken a job as book-keeper for the Champion Farm Equipment Company in Springfield, who are growing and have plans to move production to Chicago. Being the entrepreneur, like his father, he reported to the draft board that his company is doing its part for the war effort by boosting agriculture and manufacturing telegraph equipment to supply the Union armies. He got an exemption for his company staff members. I truly hope, dear brother, that you will not hold this against your nephew. I have just written a letter to him, asking him to be careful and wise. I trust he will.

Your brother Sam is exempted because he is the legal guardian of a Union officer's child. You did tell me the status of an officer begins at 2nd lieutenant, but who are we to argue, right? Sam is only grateful to you for persuading him not to rush into duty.

We are all proud that you chose to serve your country. Sam and Sydney are doing a wonderful job with your young John. I wish you could see how he plays baseball! He is always a team captain. Margaret is steady and well, and sends her fond wishes. My husband, Jacob, is proud of *you as well, and is doing a masterful job in the state legislature in support of the Union. We wish the troops success in your advance upon the citadel of Vicksburg and pray for your ultimate victory.*

Affectionately,
Mary Glessner

It's so good to hear how everyone is doing. Of course, I don't hold bad feelings against John. Each person must make his own peace with God and be guided by what most purely moves him. I'm simply amazed at the creativity and imagination of these folks.

Our 78th regiment has been put on clean-up duty down at Port Hudson, south of Vicksburg, which will free the entire Mississippi River basin. Union troops have been holding the Confederates at bay in a siege of Port Hudson, and today, July 9th, is the 48th day.

The first major battle employing black troops has just ended here today under Gen. Banks. Regrettably, negro servicemen are underpaid. A white private gets $13 a month; a colored man gets $12 a month, minus $5 for clothing, only $7. Liberation is far from complete.

People at Port Hudson tell us that during the siege, they were reduced to eating rats and mules. When news arrived of Vicksburg's surrender, Gen. Franklin Gardner gives up the battle. When our navy takes over a merchant steamboat from a wealthy trader named Butler, inspectors checked his luggage and dispose of it. I take one brass luggage tag as a souvenir, inscribed, "B. J. Butler." The inspectors say Butler traded slaves along with other merchandise. I feel like throwing the tag into the Mississippi, but I keep it: one small symbol of what we mean to crush.

After Port Hudson, we're back in Bovina, but we haven't been here a week before orders come to move again to the Vicksburg vicinity with Gen. McPherson. The boys in Company E seize the moment to present Lt. Col. Greenbury Wiley with a pair of shoulder straps, fine ones, decorated in red, white, and blue. No slouches, they put on an elaborate event. It brings back Comstock, my trading friend at Vicksburg, wearing an officer's suspenders because he'd lost so much weight in the siege.

Next orders: Clinton. We are indeed a "Flying Brigade." Company C has duty near the courthouse.

We're posted where a produce wagon is selling nearby, and all eyes turn when a young woman steps up. She's well dressed, clearly no Southern belle, and she carries herself with confidence. George leans toward me. "Who is that woman?"

"Careful," I say, keeping my eyes on the officer beside her. "You're outranked here."

A Yankee colonel behind us supplies the answer. "That's Emma Hurlbut, from Connecticut. She's connected to Vicksburg headquarters. She does her part, and the men respect her."

George lets out a sigh, hopes collapsing. My attention stays on Emma, not for romance, but for what she represents. Frances surprised me as a fighter. Now here's Emma, moving among officers, earning respect in a way men pretend not to notice.

I nudge George anyway. "Your chance will come, but you've got to be careful not to do anything unwise." Then, over my shoulder, "Thanks, Colonel." I look at George again. I've got to watch this kid.

Clinton isn't a pretty place, and plenty of soldiers are happy to leave it. "The most bitter secesh hole," Chaplain Stevenson calls it. Still, the 78th must stay as others move out. We're temporarily detached from Gen. Logan's division and placed under Gen. Arthur McArthur, Jr. The commander of the Clinton post, Col. Wiles, is inundated with applicants seeking passes to go to Vicksburg on business. He suspects something is off.

He's right. Many of the applicants are with the USMT, the United States Military Telegraph Corps. Those workers operate outside military standards and discipline. Reports come in of drinking on duty, missed calls, bribes taken to send personal messages.

Two decent men among them, brothers Blair and Carl Molvey, report something worse. They were offered bribes to send intelligence to the Confederate cavalry bound on attacking Sherman's supply train en route to Clinton. The Molveys refused, but the thought that others might not turns my stomach.

Those spies tell the Confederate cavalry we have only one regiment holding Clinton, ours. Sherman warns us to be on guard and sends for reinforcements. They arrive.

When the rebels advance, they're met by our combined forces before they realize we're no small army. Our cavalry closes in behind them. Outnumbered, 1500 rebels surrender. Sherman arrives with munitions, rations, and supplies, including a carton of horseshoes. That's good news for my equine babies as well.

Clinton's citizens are nearly starving. A delegation asks Sherman for food. He agrees on one condition: they share with former slaves, but not Confederate soldiers. I take it as an unusually considerate action, kindness to non-combatants caught in the grind. I'm proud to see it. This engagement may not be long remembered, but it is a resounding victory for Col. Wiles and the 78th Ohio on July 16.

Once the road between Clinton and Champion's Hill is secured and kept open, we join the celebration of Col. Wiles' promotion to lieutenant colonel. Arthur McArthur Jr. leaves our regiment and moves into Col. Alexander Chambers's 17th Corps. That name sticks in my mind. I can't help wondering if there will ever be an Arthur McArthur III. McArthur says he'd name his son Douglas. Casual musings after battle are a luxury like clean socks.

Back with Gen. Logan's 3rd Army Corps, we finally get the creature comforts of rest and recuperation. We say goodbye to the boys, moving with Sherman down to Memphis in early August. The scene shifts, as it always does, when orders send us on a reconnaissance mission to Monroe, Louisiana. The fun is over.

The march is hot. We tramp through swamps where cutting blades grow up to a horse's shoulder. We clear the path by shooting rattlesnakes by the dozen. At Bayou Macon, we meet the enemy in a brisk scrimmage and take prisoners as they retreat. Our orders are to demolish their camp, but when we find it, it's deserted. We march on.

Monroe, Louisiana
August 25, 1863

My dear sister Margaret,
I received your letter here at camp. What a joy to sense your stern support of the Union's cause!
I was also glad to hear from Mary. Please reas-

sure her that I hold no ill feelings against her son John. I must tell you that in the present conflict, I seldom know from one day to the next where our regiment will be called to action. We are indeed much like a fifth wheel, or as I prefer to say, a utility outfielder in baseball. Nevertheless, our 78th Ohio is proud of our service record thus far. I feel we are doing the right thing for the nation and for humanity, doing damage only when it serves the cause of the Union, and respecting human life and property beyond our commission of war.

I have in my possession two rebel artifacts which came to me without dishonor—a CSA belt buckle from Vicksburg, and a slave runner's luggage tag from the wharf at Port Gibson. Knowing how you enjoy collecting mementos, I will keep them now, but they will be yours after the war. What I will give you at my furlough is the sliver I cut from the oak tree under which Pemberton surrendered Vicksburg. Not sure when that furlough will be, but I have resolved to reenlist, as my heart is fully in accord with the preservation of the Union.

I was wounded on the big toe, but that was back at Champion's Hill in May. I'm fine now. Please give my best to all the family. Give son John a hug for me. Pray for the troops.

Your loving brother,
William

I'm not telling Margaret I got bitten by one of those damned swamp rattles. Reeves drained the wound. No need to worry her.

Chapter Twenty-Three

Cheers greet us as we march into Monroe. The people welcome us with open amazement. They've lived like an island in a sea, never seen a Yankee soldier, knowing nothing of Vicksburg's surrender. When the Confederate government ordered them to burn cotton, they had no idea why. Their women even come into camp to help prepare our sick and wounded for transport home. That kind of decency stops me short.

Lt. Col. Wiles works closely with them. After his promotion, he was granted a leave of absence but chose to stay with the regiment. Whether that's pure goodness of heart or a fondness for working alongside Southern women—ha!—I can't say. Likely both.

It's a good thing he stayed. Some of our boys volunteer at their overcrowded hospital, and the director there can't believe we're Yankees. We carry almost no identification—just names scratched into belt buckles or wooden tags worn around the neck in case we're killed or wounded. Wiles assures the hospital staff we're real, and that settles it. The women recognize him from camp. Human compassion, cutting clean across enemy lines.

Isn't that the greater reality?

We don't have long to linger in this rare calm. Now we learn why we're in Monroe. Sherman needs a clear corridor to move troops from Memphis across central Mississippi to Chattanooga. Our role is to create a diversion at Canton, drawing rebel units away from the transfer route.

Canton sits deep in one of the Confederacy's most oppressive enclaves. It's home to the flamboyant Earl Van Dorn and to Confederate President Jefferson Davis's plantation. Railroads, saloons, swaggers, and everything that goes with them. Walking the streets, I spot a large sign:

```
IT IS A MISDEMEANOR TO GALLOP A HORSE,
MARE, OR MULE, ON ANY STREET OR ALLEY
```

We pass a barn where colored folks are holding a hoe-down —music, laughter, dancing. About half a dozen white townsmen stand outside shouting, "No nigger parties!" A couple of us ask if they truly mean to stop it.

"Yup!" one old secesh blurts. "I posted it in the town newspaper, too!"

It seems they'd rather crush a harmless celebration than risk those same people joining Yankee columns and costing them more property. That barn dance may be the only breath of joy these people can claim under their oppression. I offer a silent blessing: Dance while you can. Soon enough, you'll be dancing free.

We tear up Confederate mills near Canton and march out on October 17th. Pulling apart mills feels more useful than torching courthouses, but no one's asking my opinion on strategy.

Orders send us to check an enemy camp at a place that sounds like "Bald Cheater." I keep turning the name over, unsure. It's a small settlement of mixed Indian population south of Jackson, near a creek. We ask a woman weaving baskets about it.

She doesn't even look up. "Bogue Chitto," she says. "Choctaw. Means big, fast-flowing creek."

Big or not, the skirmish there is mild and quickly over. We move on.

Gen. Logan moves on as well, leaving the 3rd Army Division to take command of the 15th. We welcome Zanesville's own Mortimer Leggett to replace him.

Sooner or later, excitement always settles back into the ordinary. Thanksgiving becomes a national holiday. President Lincoln issues a proclamation setting it for November 26, 1863. Gen. Leggett asks for volunteers to fetch turkeys, and Ted Szewzyski nearly jumps out of his boots. "I will! I will!"

He returns with his friends hauling sacks of kicking birds. Before long, the turkeys roast and camp turns raucous. A lone farmer steps into the middle of the celebration, asking to see "the man in charge." Gen. Leggett wipes his mouth.

"Are you here for payment?" he asks, then calls Ted forward.

"Private Szewzyski, can you prove these aren't this man's turkeys?"

Ted grins. "Yes, sir. If they were his, I'd have taken them all."

The farmer laughs. "It's all right. You left one fine gobbler for the missus and me. Enjoy your feast, boys."

Canton, Mississippi
October 29, 1863

My dear sister Margaret,

I hope you had a fine Thanksgiving. We surely did. How glad I am to know that the Restored Government of Virginia is about to separate legally from secessionist Virginia. We'll have our own representatives in Congress. God bless our new governor, Francis Pierpont.

Thank you, dear sister, for your letter. It took a month to reach me, but these days one is grateful for the smallest mercy. How delightful to hear my son John won a spelling bee. Please ask Sydney to reward him well. I'll increase the money I send to cover it.

I was sitting with George and some of the boys, playing poker, when I was summoned at once to report to my Corps Commander. They gave no reason, and I began searching through my misdeeds.

Instead, Gen. Leggett commended my service and informed me I had been commissioned as a 2nd Lieutenant. I can now be legitimately classed as an officer—tell Sam.

There was no muster-in ceremony, as Gen. Sherman put it on hold. That suits me fine. George threw a small celebration with spirits foraged from a secesh steamboat. He's getting accustomed to the *war's hazards. Please tell his family he's well, as am I.*

Fondly,
Your adoring brother,
William

I keep the folks informed. It steadies them—and us—should fortune turn bad. I'm glad I mailed that letter in time.

We greet New Year's Day, 1864, the same way we ended the last—tramping through swamp mud up to our knees, gallinippers whining, snakes sliding away at our boots. Brand-new year. Same old swamps. We're bound for Monroeville, Louisiana, a staging ground to join Sherman on his Meridian expedition. If luck holds, we'll arrive by January 5th, the day we may re-enlist for three more years. Those who do will be classed as veterans and granted furlough. The thought of home lifts everyone's spirits.

Sherman, newly arrived from Memphis, has other plans. Always pressing while the iron's hot, he intends to scorch what remains of Mississippi. To do it, he'll take our 17th Corps and his 16th Division on the Meridian expedition before releasing veterans for furlough. We step off on February 1st. That night, I sit with George in his tent.

"I'm signing up," I say. "You?"

George rubs his stubbled jaw. "I will, too. I want to be seen as a true soldier in Sherman's March to the Sea and help end this war."

I study him. "Am I looking at the same George Hall?"

"Maybe not," he says. "I still hate the thought of wrecking homes and property. But marching beside you matters, if we live that long."

"If we live that long," I echo.

Chapter Twenty-Four

We march out of Canton in the dark. The February air is cool and crisp. Somewhere an owl hoots under the waning moon. Sherman has placed us under Gen. Stephen Hurlbut, an understudy of McClernand and a hard-drinking son of a Unitarian minister (happily, not related to Emma). Under Hurlbut's command, we move with McPherson's 17th Corps and Ed Winslow's cavalry toward the railroad bridge near Bolton.

At 4:00 a.m., a courier gallops in from Winslow and skids to a halt, dust flying. Winslow and McPherson have engaged the former Indian fighter Wirt Adams on the northeast slope of Champion's Hill. After a skirmish, the Yankees push him back to his main line west of Baker's Creek.

Hurlbut brings us in from the north, with McPherson pressing from the west, and Winslow's cavalry from the south. Adams falls back again toward the Walton plantation. His men stall at the creek crossing, leaving Confederate infantry exposed. McPherson's troops surge across the open field, but rebel cannons rake them until Adams's men finish crossing Baker's Creek.

Just after dawn, McPherson attacks, and our division goes in. A cannon shot takes Pvt. Taylor Geary of the 78th in the head, blasting half of it away. The same shot fractures Col. Joseph Cosan's skull and rips through Pvt. Hiram Fogle's shoulder before ricocheting off to disable his gun. McPherson himself steps in with an artillery crew to work a brand-new 20-pound Parrott gun.

Overwhelmed, the rebels fall back into the woods.

We pursue and plunge into a tight, punishing fight, close enough to see faces, not close enough for bayonets. The realization hits hard: it's like fighting your own people. Same boots, same weapons, same resolve. Americans killing Americans.

The thought almost costs me, but I keep my head. Someone forces his way toward me through the press. I know him by his gait before I see his face. Braddox. Smoke still curls above his head from the shot he's fired. He's already reloading, ahead of me. I reach for my cartridge box, knowing I'm too late, when...

WHOOSH. A tomahawk spins past me and buries itself in the tree beside him. Braddox howls, clutching his head, and goes down. His bushwhacker gang drags him off through the smoke, coughing curses. It feels like a violent dream.

Hoofbeats thunder behind me. I glimpse a one-legged rider on a small Appaloosa. Pasquale. Only he could throw so true— spare a life and still take an ear.

The fighting breaks off as Gen. Hurlbut calls us in. Adams has regrouped on a ridge two miles off—Tombstone. He faces our combined forces. It looks like we have him. Sherman orders Winslow's cavalry behind the enemy. Adams knows he'll be surrounded and—yes—he withdraws.

As we leave Canton, we burn what remains from earlier fires. The residents now call it Chimneyville, for the lone chimneys standing in the rubble. Sherman presses his march onward through Mississippi.

That night, George and I lie on dry leaves under a sky thick with stars.

"I've heard talk about Lincoln finding a new Secretary of War," George says.

"Right," I say. "He had to 'promote' Halleck out."

George props himself on an elbow. "Who do you think he'll choose?"

Good. He's thinking strategy. "Irvin McDowell, George McClellan, Nathaniel Lyon, Joseph Hooker, plenty of possibilities."

George snorts. "You're baiting me. Who do you really think?"

"Ulysses S. Grant."

"Exactly," George says. "And who'll command the Western Theater?"

I roll toward him. "Could be Daniel McCook Jr., Grant's old law partner."

"You're doing it again. It's William Tecumseh Sherman."

"You're right. No doubt."

George sits up, yawning loud enough to startle a crow. "And I'll bet he's not just reinforcing Chattanooga. He's sweeping Mississippi like a dress rehearsal for his March to the Sea."

"Good thinking."

That's how it unfolds. Sherman charts a 150-mile course across Mississippi, throwing diversions at Mobile and elsewhere to scatter the enemy.

We leave destruction behind—bridges, sawmills, railroads, military works. No civilians are killed, but towns are left without food or water for days. That troubles George, and me as well. Starvation skirts the edge of acceptable force. Women haul river water in pails.

We pass half-built earthworks abandoned at our approach, campfires left burning. The road is littered with what isn't worth carrying—broken wagon parts, dead horses and mules, empty cartridge boxes, discarded blankets, forever-tossed playing cards. It feels like moving through ghost towns with the ghosts still watching.

At Decatur, we expect resistance from Ambrose Hill at Big Chunky River. There's none—only felled trees and a wrecked wagon bridge. Our engineers clear the road. We destroy the railroad and its bridge over the Okatibbee and burn piles of cotton. Sherman says they'd only slow us. Officers call our wagons "incumbrances." Artillerymen call them "Uncle Sam's chariots."

Noise rises along the line as civilians and negroes fall in behind us, helping keep the road open. A lone negro boy— maybe twelve—asks for food. When given hardtack, he begs to join the army.

"What's your name?" I ask.

"Edmond."

"With your family?"

"Gray Jackets killed my Pa. Ma ain't strong 'nuff. She says, 'Root hogger die.'"

The phrase stops me. I ask Howard what it means.

"You'd know if you were a farm boy," he says. "Turn hogs loose; they fend for themselves. Means you survive or you don't."

Enlistment age is eighteen, but younger boys already serve —stretcher bearers, surgeon's helpers, drummers, fifers, couriers. No one turns Edmond away, so he stays with the 78th.

George takes him, teaching him to ride. The boy shows

promise. I picture my son John back in Zanesville and try not to linger on it.

Decatur, Mississippi
February 25th, 1864

Dear Sydney and Sam,

I feel the need to write to you today, and this brief moment grants the time to do so. You've heard of an occasional young boy becoming attached to a regiment. But today we experienced an unusual case. The little fellow won a place in our hearts and in the army by his brave handling of a deplorable situation. As we were marching through Mississippi, a band of negroes fell in behind us seeking refuge from their enslavement. "Edmond," as he calls himself, has experienced the death of his father and the disability of his mother. In practicality, he is an orphan. He appears bright and wants to be of service to our cause. I cannot but think of my own son, whom you care for so admirably, my Johnny.

We Union soldiers often call the Confederate soldiers "Johnnies," from the common expression, "Billy Yank & Johnny Reb." The sad truth is that often the Billy and Johnny are actual brothers from a border state of divided loyalties, like Ohio. When I hear of rebel soldiers being called

"Johnnies," I cringe to think of my own son, who you are so kindly taking care of until my return. Please do not reveal to him my anguish over this, but know that the issue is but one of the many trials and tribulations to be endured in these difficult times.

We are in Decatur, a suburb of Meridian. We're supposed to combine forces with William Sooy Smith, but he is not here. Our corps with Gen. Hurlbut will move on to the east without him in the morning. Sherman is staying behind to wait for one of the regiments. He will retire for the night in an abandoned house. I don't know where we'll sleep tonight, probably in some other house.

Oh! The bugler is sounding Gen. Hurlbut's call! Something is afoot. My best wishes to the entire family.

To the Union,

William

Chapter Twenty-Five

Night has fallen, and there's no time for sleeping in Decatur. We're ordered to move on. As we march through the dark, Jose Fleisher whispers, "Will, do you think Wirt Adams knows we're heading to Meridian?"

"It's possible," I say, drawing a slow breath. "Sooy Smith never showed up in Decatur—that's a bad sign. Too many questions. If Adams's men caught Sooy, is it safe to leave Sherman here? And how strong are the defenses at Fort Meridian?"

"Or," Jose says, "is there a rotten-apple counterspy feeding the Confederates our numbers and movements? Anyone seen Hiram Castleberry lately?"

At first light, a courier gallops in, face set like stone. "Sherman was nearly kidnapped in Decatur," he reports. "The only thing that saved him was the pickets and the 25th Wisconsin hauling him down from the second floor. Men and wagons outside the house took damage."

My breath catches, thinking of what those wagoners must have endured.

Our nerves are raw as we approach the Meridian stockade.

My heart pounds; even a grasshopper vaulting through the grass makes me jump. To our shock—and relief—we find only a handful of defenders. Sherman has fooled them, diverting their strength to Mobile. Their commander, the Episcopal bishop Leonidas Polk, ordered an evacuation, according to the skeleton crew left behind. We carry out Sherman's orders, destroying the stockade, depots, storehouses, arsenal, camps, and hospitals.

That last part gnaws at me. Not long ago, we were volunteering at a Confederate hospital, and they were binding our wounds. No one speaks of it now. A silence settles, each man swallowing his share of guilt.

Still wondering what became of Sooy Smith, we turn back toward Vicksburg. "Move it!" someone barks. At the Canton depot, we load prisoners onto railcars. "Butternuts," a sergeant snaps, "homespun, not gray. You'll see mills making Confederate gray when we hit Atlanta. Gotta smash 'em."

A few miles down the line, escaped slaves tell us Sooy Smith blundered into Forrest's cavalry and was routed. There's that name again—Forrest. We should never have let him slip out of Fort Donelson.

Sherman assigns several regiments, with Col. Wiles, to escort the human cargo onto a supply train through Vicksburg. For volunteering, we're allowed to keep Edmond.

Before leaving Canton, word comes that Ulysses S. Grant has been appointed to a post not held since George Washington—General-in-Chief of the Armies of the United States, March 9, 1864. Sherman succeeds him as commander of the Western Theater.

"I told you so," George says.

"You could've won a bet," I say.

"You think anyone would've backed someone else?" he laughs.

With the expedition complete—successful in Sherman's

eyes—he grants all who re-enlisted a rail pass home on furlough.

"Home to Zanesville!" George and I shout together.

Before we leave camp, we make a point of saying goodbye to Edmond, promising we'll see him when we return.

He flashes a grin. "Lord willin' and the creek don't rahz!"

Howard translates at our puzzled looks. "Means you'll keep your promise unless God Himself or the Creek Indians stop you."

At mail call, I get a letter. I save it for the train.

Louisville, Kentucky
April 6th, 1864

Dear Lt. Willian,

My life has taken many turns since you left me at the contraband camp at Corinth after helping Frances Elizabeth Quinn. After a while, I decided to follow her path and get myself into the army at Fort Southworth in Louisville, disguised as a male.

I was at a Whiskey Row tavern in Louisville and met a man in uniform. We had a couple of drinks. I told him about you, and he said, "I know Lt. William Laughlin." Lo and behold, I was not talking to a man; I was talking with Frances Quinn still impersonating male soldiers! We started exchanging our stories, and a handsome black Union captain from the 44th USCT introduced himself to us "boys" as Capt. Sinclair

Breckenridge. He suggested a ride on the Ohio River on his small boat.

A much larger vessel sideswiped us, causing our boat to capsize. Breckenridge told us to cling to the gunwales of the boat, and he would swim to get help. Firemen fished us out of the water and transported us to the hospital to be checked out. Wrote up our fake names for disorderly conduct. The hospital crew discovered we were female, and when Capt. Breckenridge came to visit the now "soldier girls," he took an interest in me.

We fell in love, and now I'm Mrs. Sinclair Breckenridge.

Fanny Liz went to her surrogate home in LaMoille. There she heard for the first time that her brother Tommy had been killed at Shiloh. She again managed to get herself back into the ranks under the name of Elmer Reno. She asked me to wish you fond regards. I send fond regards as well, for all the kindness you showed her and to me.

Love,
Jamie

I kiss the letter, lower my hands, and stare out the train window. Well, I'll be a son of a gun. I never expected to hear from Jamie. You never know the mark you leave on someone. And Frances, still unstoppable. I ought to write "Elmer Reno" at once. But where in the world is her unit?

Chapter Twenty-Six

With a blast of its whistle, the train groans out of Vicksburg Station on a cloudy morning in late March. I'm as keyed up as before any battle. So eager to see Johnny—he must be a handsome ten-year-old by now. Finally, I can thank Sam and Sydney in person for all they've done for him. I'm just as eager to see my sister Margaret, faithful with her letters, and my sister Mary, who taught me so much about caring for horses...and women. Ha!

The train left Vicksburg at 7:38 a.m., and it's been a long ride. The brakeman screeches us to a halt.

"Where are we?" George asks, barely awake.

"Indianapolis Union Station. Overnight stop before Columbus. We're changing trains."

As we step down, a crowd on the platform waves a huge WELCOME sign—cheering, dancing, chanting, "USA! USA!"

"Who are they?" George asks.

"A delegation of citizens," the conductor beams. "They'll escort you to a church nearby. Hot supper waiting. Border state, you know. Folks don't hold back."

We're up early and rolling again. Columbus Union Station is quieter, but the conductor tells us the ladies in Zanesville are preparing a grand reception.

"A grand reception!" George says. "That's respect!"

I feel different. I'm done rattling along on military transport.

"I'll stop here in Columbus," I tell him. "Eat real Ohio food at my own pace, then catch the next train to Zanesville."

Columbus Union Station smells like a horse barn. Hacks and carriages crowd the lobby. People surge in every direction. I claim a stool at the lunch counter—anything but sow-belly and beans.

I forget, for a moment, how much southern Ohio leans secesh. I'm reminded fast enough.

A knot of young rowdies takes offense at my uniform.

"Hey, Joe, see that nigger-lover?"

"Maybe he needs a lesson in states' rights."

One shoves my back, trying to start something.

Then a woman appears. About my age. Neatly dressed. Dark, steady eyes. She spins the stool beside me and sits.

"There you are, Wally! Thanks for saving me a seat!"

The rowdies fall silent. Old rule—don't act coarse when women are watching.

I've survived hunger and shellfire but never been rescued by a woman!

She suggests we leave.

"I'll tell you where once we're outside.

"You like chili with real meat?"

"Hankering for it."

"Then St. Elmo's Fire. Best in town."

The place is cozy, done up in a South American style with palms and toucans. I order chili con carne. She gets ham and cheese on rye, coffee for both of us.

"Thanks for stepping in back there," I tell her. "A fight would've drawn a crowd. Who knows where it'd end."

"Happy to help. You're saving the nation. The least I can do is save you from a brawl."

"William Laughlin."

"Louise Higson." She brushes auburn hair aside. "I lost my husband last year. Pony Express runner. I was at the station seeing my brother Alexander off—he's headed for Hampton from Zanesville."

She speaks plainly, without asking for sympathy. I like that. Her eyes don't waver.

"I'm sorry, Louise. I lost my wife, too. Mary—stroke, two years ago."

Our food arrives. She shares half her sandwich.

Then it hits me.

"You're from Zanesville. That's where I'm headed. Let me see you home—I'll hire a carriage."

We linger long past the meal. Coffee keeps coming. She tells me about her quiet corner of town. I tell her about the Glessner place and my family.

I pay the bill, tip generously, and feel the diamond ring in my pocket. Maybe I did tip heavily. All the while, she keeps brushing her hair back, smiling just a little. There's something here.

On the train, sitting side by side, her face goes still.

"Something wrong?"

"Just thinking."

"About?"

"My brother Alex is taking the train to Hampton to receive military training at Fort Monroe. He is following our uncle, Sgt. Stephen Higson, who went into military service. Our family has its roots in Richmond. Uncle Steve joined Gen. John Pope's new Army of Virginia because he wanted to drive the rebels out of Richmond."

"An honorable pursuit. I knew Gen. Pope, back when we fought together at Corinth. Why are you contemplative about it?"

"Uncle Steve was in the Battle of Culpeper County against Maj. Gen. Thomas 'Stonewall' Jackson at Cedar Mountain back in August of '62. Gen. Pope had arrived from D. C. less than two weeks before the Cedar Mountain battle. Pope barely knew his troops, and they barely knew him."

"I think his first order was issued from what he called Headquarters in the Saddle."

"Yes. He was giving orders, not from his horse, but by telegraph out of Washington. Lincoln was utilizing him as an advisor while the War Department was looking for a General-In-Chief, who would become Ulysses Grant, you know. Pope is a brilliant military strategist, even though he is given to self-glorification."

This woman knows a lot about the war. About the arrogance of some generals and the terrors to face in combat!

"And didn't his soldiers make a joke of his Headquarters in the Saddle?"

"They did. Uncle Steve says they joked that he must have his brains where most people have their hindquarters. Anyhow, Uncle Steve was in the artillery group under Alpheus Williams, the artillery that shot CSA Gen. Charles Winder."

"Stonewall Jackson's second-in-command."

"Yes, but that's not my concern. It's the horror of what that shell did! Winder was surveying the battle through his binoculars and giving range adjustments to his artillery crew, who were manning a Parrott gun. The soldiers of the battery next to Winder were lying prone. Nobody could hear orders above the roar of the shooting and the trees spitting all around!

"One gunner crawls to Winder and asks him to repeat the adjustment order. He stands up and cups his hands to his mouth, preparing to yell louder. And just then, the Union shell rips him! Right between his left arm and his torso! It tore most of the flesh from his arm and ripped his side open all the way to his spine! He fell to the ground quivering and died unaided, except by the chaplain."

"War is hell."

"Yes, and I think Uncle Steve will never get over that incident. I wouldn't want my brother to go through an experience like that. You probably know that Pope's army had only a temporary victory that day, and April 9th ended in a rout of the Union in favor of Stonewall Jackson. But the *Zanesville Courier* touted it, encouraged by Pope's famous boasting, as though their small win was a major battle victory.

"In truth, William," she continues, "Pope had only repelled one corps, the 21st Virginia, which spurred a failed attack. I clipped the news report to caution my brother on how things can go wrong, even if they start out favorably. The article in the *Zanesville Courier*, in fact, shows serious Union casualties. Here.

"In the battle of Culpeper, we lost but one general, who was left behind in a ditch, spiked. Several of the brave having been killed, the gun was not lost, but by changing over our position for the night, under fire of the enemy's sharpshooters, Col. Chapman of Massachusetts was shot in the breast and is probably dead. Lt. Col. Stone fell with enemy wounds. Major Blake also fell and is a prisoner if alive. Adjutant Smith is wounded or dead. Major Savage of Company 53, Massachusetts believed to be killed, as well as many of the commanding leaders.

"And the list goes on. Does that look like a victory? And you know how John Pope continued on, seventeen days later, to face Stonewall Jackson at 2nd Bull Run, and ended that battle losing 14,000 casualties."

"Dreadful losses happen in any battle, win or lose. But I do share your care in cautioning your brother, and how moral guilt can take over a fighting man's head."

"Alex ignored the news clipping and gave it back to me at the station. I want to give it to you, William, to remind you to use moral discernment in whatever you're faced with in this war.

"Louise, I promise I will not ignore that danger. I fear for my Johnny the way you fear for Alex. Thank you! I will keep your clipping to remind me of how much you care."

She grips my hand. I pull her close, and we kiss. A long while.

The train comes to a halt at Zanesville Station, exhausting steam. I hail a wagon driver to see her home. During the ride, we're making plans to meet again. "Tomorrow's Saturday. I will visit Johnny and the family and spend time with them. Then I can come, and we'll do something on Sunday. How does that sound?"

"Sounds good, William, but I am committed to going to church."

"Catholic?"

"No, Episcopal. You?"

"Presbyterian. I could pick you up, and you can attend church with my family," I propose. "They would be delighted to meet you."

"They might not take to me, William. What then?"

"Then, after church, you and I will play with Johnny. I am certain he will take to you!"

"You cover all the bases, don't you?" she says, brushing her hair back with that irresistible smile. "Nine-thirty, William."

"Great! I'll be at your place at nine-twenty."

The good horse trots as Louise directs the driver directly to her house, a pretty little bungalow at the edge of town. I thank the driver, asking him to wait. "It's getting late, William," she says. "Better go see your folks. I'm happy for you, seeing your son." We climb down from the carriage. She throws her arms around my neck. A close embrace and a long, long kiss.

"You know something, Louise?" I say, "Something tells me it would be very pleasing for us to spend time together during my furlough. And it's not just a casual acquaintance for me, Loise. It's a deep feeling within."

She brushes her hair back, "Same here, William, same here. After all, I've got to keep finding places to feed you chili, William." Then, affectionately, she jokes, "I could call you Chilli Will!"

My solo carriage ride home provides a time to reflect. There's something about this woman. She is deeply involved in this war, yet she seems to care greatly about me. The driver senses my soliloquy. "You're in love, Mister. I can tell!"

"That I am, sir. At first, it was a cordial exchange. Now it's the real thing." I pay him his fare plus a good tip. "Pick me up on Sunday?"

"On time, guaranteed!" says the driver.

Sunday is here, and we're sitting in the pews, brothers Alexander and Sam with Sydney, Mary and Jacob, and Margaret, with Louise, Johnny, and me—quite a delegation! I hope we're not overwhelmingly conspicuous, but I'm afraid we are. The family's acquaintance with Louise has gone well, and Johnny has taken to her completely.

The day moves on, and we're at a boat dock, Louise, Johnny, and I, to enjoy a delightful day fishing in Lake Erie.

He's catching more than Louise and me together! We'll make visits to Sam, Sydney and my sisters a bit later.

At the Glessner homestead, I reach into my wallet and present my loyal sister Margaret with the wood cut from the oak where Pemberton surrendered Vicksburg. She is overjoyed. Johnny is excited to hear the story. I must confess, I'm getting a bit tearful myself. Being the patriot that she is, Margaret places the wood silver immediately in a pin box for safekeeping. Then, she carefully arranges the pin box in her bay window, along with a miniature cannon, a U.S. flag, a bust of President Lincoln, and placards of unidentified navy personnel portraits.

The days pass too quickly. True to our plans, we have spent most of my furlough deepening our relationship. Her small home has become a haven for our intimacy.

We're all back in church, the whole lot. The pastor, Rev. Ben Thornton, is holding my attention with a sermon about laborers in the vineyard, a message that it's never too late to do the right thing. It's our last Sunday before I return to my regiment.

Louise reaches into her purse and, with a blank face, passes me a little card during the worship service. It depicts an angel surrounded by baroque flowers, with the inscription:

The night's getting late, and soon we must part,
Pray tell me, have I an interest yet in your heart?

I squeeze her hand in assent. After the service, my family folks head home, leaving Louise and me to linger in the churchyard. "You are getting sentimental about my returning to the war, aren't you?"

"You know I am!" she affirms.

"So, I've got something for you, Louise. Give me your left hand."

"What's this?" she says. Somewhat befuddled, but blushing, she stretches out her hand.

I remove the ring from my pocket, the diamond I've been keeping for such a time as this. I place it on her finger. Thank God it fits! "Like it?"

"Oh, William, I love it! But you shouldn't have spent the money!"

"I spent none. It was given to me."

She comes back teasing, "What girl broke your engagement?"

"My brother Sam and his wife sent it to me long ago. It was Mary's. Sydney had a sense I might need it sometime."

Without another word, she throws her arms around my neck. Then, as our lips meet, she says, laughing, "We should not be kissing in the churchyard."

"Then we can do it inside! And I'll ask Rev. Thornton to bless our union."

"Right here and now, without a marriage license?'

"There's no telling what tomorrow holds."

Chapter Twenty-Seven

Pastor Thornton is casually chatting with the last stragglers out of church. We wait, fidgeting off to one side. When the folks walk out the door, he approaches with a smile and an extended hand.

"And a good morning, indeed, to you, Lieutenant Laughlin. And so nice to see you again, Miss Higson. I'm imagining your pleasure with the well-deserved furlough, sir."

Louise, asserting, speaks up, "Pastor Thorton, William and I would like you to bless our devotion to each other through a ceremony of Holy Union." I feel her arm tightening around my waist. The diamond ring sparkles.

Rev. Thornton lifts his fists together to his mouth, deep in thought. He breathes out a great exhale and asks, "When do you return to your regiment, William?"

"The six o'clock train tomorrow morning."

"Well!" he says, with a confident look. "We understand the vicissitudes of war, don't we? To me, it's clear that the Lord cannot wait another minute. Let's step to the front of the sanctuary."

Once settled, he begins, "William and Louise, you come before God..." He says it so casually; I've been coming before God in earnest on each battlefield!

He is continuing with solemn prayer, "William and Louise have chosen to commit themselves to a life of loving faithfulness..." I will be away for so long, but faithfully we'll take it for granted, I'm absolutely sure.

Now a scripture. Something about "Arise, my love and come away..." I didn't know intimate stuff like that was in the Bible!

We say some simple vows. A warm and solid sense of rightness flows over me as she speaks, "I, Louise, give myself to you, William..." And also, as I speak, "to love and to cherish 'til death do us part."

Rev. Thornton speaks the closing announcement that we are "life partners in Holy Union." Then he interrupts our kissing embrace with, "Do you want to jump over a broom, as many of my couples do?"

"We'll pass," Louise says, brushing back her hair. Those dark eyes shine.

I'm profoundly moved. What we've done feels—somehow —truer than any formal rite. Louise tells me she feels the same.

Morning comes too soon. She rides me to Zanesville Station.

"Take good care of yourself, William," she says, kissing me and slipping a folded paper into my breast pocket.

I hold her until the conductor calls, "All aboard!" We keep hold of each other as I climb the steps. From the window, I wave. She blows a kiss from the platform. When will I see her again?

After changing trains in Columbus, I glance at the café where I first met her. No hoodlums this time. The train rolls on through Indianapolis and back toward Vicksburg. As the cars sway, my thoughts drift to women.

This war is relentless; killing, being hunted, always alert. It frays a man's nerves. A man works hard just to keep body and soul together. My furlough with Louise has sharpened my sense of what proper regard for women truly means. The 78th Ohio is admirable that way. I know of only one exception. Sgt. Arthur M. Carty was court-martialed for assaulting a teenage girl in a farmhouse. Nothing like that ever touched me with Louise. Our intimacy grew naturally from shared trust and the weight of war. For that, I am grateful.

Chapter Twenty-Eight

"Create havoc!" The colonel's voice shatters the sunrise, jolting sleepy eyes and straining ears. The order is simple, brutal, and straight from Grant: destroy anything that serves the enemy. No questions.

The men mutter in grim excitement. It isn't just nerves: will Johnston himself be "a thing that serves the enemy"? The weight of it settles on all of us. Word spreads fast—Sherman now commands three armies, and we're marching into Georgia with Atlanta as the prize. The 78th will be with Gen. George Thomas, pushing hard against Cleburne's defenses around Marietta.

The talk of old raids and locomotives dies as we shoulder our gear. I'm charged with the challenge. George is settling into the strain of army life, and I'm grateful for it.

We've just knocked out the garrison controlling Cleburne's earthworks. Gen. Thomas presses on, deploying "Fighting Joe" Hooker across an open field, and here we meet resistance. Cleburne has blocked us with sharpened logs thrust outward. Mounted officers, cavalry, and even the wagon train all stall.

We fight through the afternoon into twilight with no gain. Rebels set up artillery by a small wooden church called Gilgal. Because he wants open ground, a Texas captain tears the church down log by log. As we advance, our men are shot down. Nothing to boast of.

The next afternoon, we face the southern rise of the Appalachian Ridge, planted like a wall before Atlanta. We'll see if it holds.

Gen. Schofield's Army of the Ohio moves toward Lost Mountain, gaining a position to fire into Cleburne's works. Heavy guns are dragged up and pound the line.

The enemy's left buckles when Col. Brownlow of the Pioneer Corps drives them off Lost Mountain, opening a wide view toward Atlanta. The rebels fall back again, toward Kennesaw Mountain.

A misunderstanding flares between Hooker and Sherman. Sherman orders Hooker to outflank Johnston at Kolb's Farm. It fails. Sherman then orders a frontal attack, worse than Hooker's. Too many officers' squabbles and jealousies. Talk of "a more perfect Union"—far from perfect.

We shake it off and, with fewer numbers, move to Kennesaw Mountain, 1,800 feet rising beyond Marietta. The sight alone is daunting. We're twenty miles from Atlanta.

At the base, Johnston has laid a seven-mile line of defenses. Sherman must choose—flank well-equipped troops or strike the center. Scuttlebutt reaches us.

"Did you hear?" Jose rushes in. "Gen. Thomas told Sherman to hit the left flank."

"That could be needled on the right," Szewzyski adds, then looks at me. "Your take, Will?"

"Left flank," I say, "but I fear a frontal blow down the middle—the kind of bravado we saw at Lost Mountain."

George arrives breathless. "I passed the commanders' tent.

Two spies are pushing Sherman to pull out all the stops—frontal attack, destroy Johnston now. It smells wrong."

"You sure?" Jose asks, ramming his musket.

"George remembers what he hears verbatim," I say.

Szewzyski frowns. "Did you recognize them?"

"Backs turned," George says. "Didn't know the voice."

"That's too bad," Ted says. "You're good with voices."

Before the words fade, a high squeal streaks away from the tent. We snap our heads as the hind end of a pig vanishes into the crowd.

"Grab that pig," Jose says. "Might be sabotage." Too late.

No time to wonder if it's Bowser. "Attention!"

Sherman's adjutant rises. "The plan is set. Frontal attack. Gen. Daniel McCook Jr.'s brigade will lead." He spits tobacco.

The lines curve like a great C: Confederates on the inner rise, Union below. Sherman on our right, McPherson on our left. The 78th Ohio, under George H. Thomas, stands at the center—the Dead Angle, a bare swath of grass. We face Cheatham's division. In open ground, we carry the weight of Grant's "now or never."

Sherman orders the attack at dawn on June 27th—98,000 to Johnston's 49,000. Many take comfort in the numbers. We don't. The spies' message feels like sabotage, and pigs don't wander freely through packed camps.

Gen. Daniel McCook Jr., Sherman's law partner, charges on a white stallion, sword up, shouting for surrender with curses. A shot takes his left lung. He falls, and his brigade breaks. The Army of the Cumberland must fill the gap in blazing heat against a timbered fortress.

Before we arrived, Johnston forced enslaved workers to dig trenches and raise parapets across the slopes, fifty howitzers hauled uphill, saplings felled and sharpened downhill.

"Not even a rabbit gets through that," Jose says.

My gut tightens at the thought of those workers, laboring against their own freedom, unpaid.

Shot, shell, and musket tear into us. A round whips past my ear like a giant mosquito. Gen. Logan brings reinforcements—no breach. Wave after wave falls. Men writhe across the grass. Some climb close enough that the enemy hurls rocks.

The heat is intolerable, like a foundry. No shade. Men drop from sunstroke, mouths open. Dry grass ignites from exploding shells. Men burn.

Then CSA Col. William Martin of the 15th Arkansas stands on a parapet with a white flag. We freeze. Not surrender. He shouts, "This is butchery!" and calls a brief cease-fire.

Both sides collect the wounded and dead. Coffee trades for tobacco. Then the bugle calls us back. Blue, gray, and butternut streaked with crimson. A strange war.

After one day: 3,000 Union casualties, 1,000 Confederate. Gen. Thomas urges Sherman to flank and move on. Enough have died. No victory yet.

Sherman refuses. Five more days.

The wrong choice. Not learned from Lost Mountain. We believe Sherman was misled by the spies.

At last, Gen. John M. Schofield pulls a brilliant feint at the Confederate right, drawing men off, and Sherman slips through the weak opposite flank. Schofield follows, barely opposed.

That night, the Confederates abandon Kennesaw, leaving some asleep in their trenches. Our clean-up finds them. One wakes to Szewzyski looming.

"Oh no! Oh no!"

Seeing a military uniform, he exhales. "I thought it was a swamp ape!"

"Swamp ape?" Szewzyski asks. We laugh.

"Like a Sasquatch. Saw one in Florida. Shot at it. Kept walking."

"Bourbon and gunpowder," I say. "You're drinking bat shit." He nearly retches, then realizes he's captured. He curses his commander, relieved all the same.

We find two dazed men from the Bureau of Military Information, their pins missing.

"Knocked cold," they say. "IDs stolen."

"Confederates," one mutters.

"Or rebels posing as Union intelligence personnel," I say. "And I think I know one."

"Who?"

"Let Gen. Thomas handle it. Come, Reeves will check you."

On the road, George asks softly, "The pig, was it a clue?"

"Yes." Dead Angle will not leave me.

Because the losses were so great, Sherman was fortunate to flank Johnston and keep us moving. Johnston evacuates Kennesaw in heavy rain, falling back toward Atlanta.

A Union defeat, yet a strategic success. Schofield's move forces another retreat. July 2nd, 1864; nearly a year since Vicksburg.

Chapter Twenty-Nine

A tattered bunch we are, skirting the mountain's edge, and George is limping badly, his whole right side lurching.

"Hey, old buddy, what's wrong? Your leg?"

"Minie ball grazed my calf," he says. "The right one. One of those Texans."

I grab my medical kit and look. "You're dramatizing, George. This isn't a graze—it's a damned gash."

I clean and bandage it. The damage is worse than it first looked—torn flesh hanging loose, bleeding steadily. It makes me shudder to think how close he came to losing the leg if the bone had shattered.

I patch him well enough for Surgeon Reeves to see him at the next watering stop, where he's checking those intelligence officers.

"You're riding with me on the wagon. No arguing."

As we jolt along, we make a pledge on the spot: if one of us doesn't survive the war, the other will send word to his family. We seal it with a long, firm wraparound handshake.

In the middle of that solemn moment, a courier brings news

from another wing of Sherman's army near Guntown, Mississippi. Moving out from Memphis to join us, Gen. Samuel Sturgis's troops were hit by Nathan Bedford Forrest's cavalry. Forrest somehow ignited the Yankees' ordnance wagon, setting off a devastating blast.

My stomach knots at the thought. Ammunition has to stay near the center of a fight, which makes the wagon a deadly target. It takes sharp eyes at every turn.

That night, the image of the exploding wagon still burning behind my eyes, I miss the quiet steadiness of the woman I love. I find a scrap of paper and write.

Marietta, Georgia
July 3rd, 1864

My dear Louise,
I long to celebrate the Fourth with you, but you know my duty—to see this war through Bobby Lee's surrender, or at least until the next furlough. I'm certain the battle at Kennesaw Mountain will be remembered as a horror on both sides.

Words fail for what it was like: parched mouths, blistering heat, hillside cannon, musket fire, bayonets over earthworks and palisades. Gen. Sherman chose a frontal attack led by our division, despite Gen. Thomas's wise warning.

You deserve the truth. Men died by the dozens —torn apart by canister and musket fire, struck down by sunstroke. And the smell—the nauseating smell of death. My friend George Hall took a

*minie ball through his right calf. Being this close
to death teaches a man the worth of life.*

*Be brave, my dear Louise, as you must be for
your brother Alex. I pray for his safety as I
do for yours. I ache to hold you as I did in
those precious days and nights. Soon we will face
the enemy at Atlanta. The rest is in God's hands.
I must return to the march.*

Affectionately,
William

I blow a kiss to the page, as if it might carry the feeling with it, and tuck it carefully into my wallet for the next mail carrier.

My aching heart meets my rumbling belly. We've been without rations for three days. Hunger grinds us down. Then, like a small miracle, a grocer's wagon rattles toward us.

Cornbread. The driver has no idea how hungry we are, and he's stunned when soldiers swarm the wagon. Word races through the division, and soon there's a panicked crush for cornbread.

"Doesn't bother me, boys," the driver laughs. "You just helped me unload. My boss'll know I was outmanned and outgunned."

Then Sherman drops vinegar on the feast. A telegram arrives at Gen. Thomas's headquarters: "Press with vehemence at any cost of life and material."

Some of that material is us.

Sherman has learned that Johnston used enslaved labor to build two defensive lines north of the Chattahoochee. One runs from the old Smyrna campground down Concord Road to Ruff's Mill on Nickajack Creek. Sherman can't believe a general as seasoned as Johnston would risk cutting his retreat short of a major river. He orders Thomas to tell Schofield and McPherson that if we move fast, we can catch them before they cross.

We've slept on bare ground and eaten nothing but cornbread. Our bodies beg for mercy. Duty doesn't.

Unlike July Fourth at Vicksburg, our Independence Day of 1864 is a hoarse, empty-bellied charge. Sherman adopts Grant's three-pronged advance. Schofield skirts southwest toward Ruff's Mill to engage the first line.

With Gen. Thomas's Army of the Cumberland, we march on the Sandtown Road toward the river, a diversion. McPherson follows behind us, poised to strike the second line— the River Line at the Chattahoochee.

Under heavy fire, we smash through earthworks, take 150 prisoners, and drive the rebels toward the river.

Closing in along Vickery Creek, we find a cluster of mills. Roswell Mill has a French flag flying over its cupola.

"What do they make?" I ask Col. Sinnott.

"A little flour," he says, "and a lot of cotton and wool textiles under Confederate contract." He squints. "Major Garrard found gray fabric stamped CSA—uniform cloth. You know what that means."

George quotes Grant at once: "The destruction of all resources that would benefit the Confederacy." Then he hesitates. "But it's under France's flag."

"The mill boss works for Roswell King," Sinnott says. "A Frenchman. He raised the flag, hoping for neutrality. This is Georgia, not a French embassy."

400 mill workers are rounded up and charged with treason. Nearly all are women. We're told they're French immigrants who fled Mexico four months ago after Juárez's army crushed the French-backed regime and executed Maximilian.

I watch how they're handled as obstacles to Sherman's 'press on' order. Not as noncombatants. Not as women fleeing persecution.

Most are barely seventeen. They own nothing but the clothes on their backs—ragged, grease-stained, factory rank. Some carry children, equally worn and thin. They don't shout like Southern belles. They look afraid.

As they pass, George notices one girl. Grease masks a young face—black hair, dark hazel eyes, high cheekbones. She reaches for his hand. He touches it gently, then the line moves on.

"What's going to happen to them?" George asks.

Sinnott answers plainly. "They'll be marched under guard to the Georgia Military Institute in Marietta. After processing, put in boxcars to Indianapolis and left to fend for themselves. The mill is destroyed."

George turns to me. "Doesn't that sound...wrong?"

"Vastly so," I say. "They deserve respect, as noncombatants, and as women. But we don't make the rules."

"Brutal," George mutters.

It leaves me wondering if there's a moral law above military necessity. I think our commanders feel it, too. Yet if we fail, doesn't slavery remain the greater wrong? God, if there's a balance, let me keep searching until I find it.

Chapter Thirty

The heat isn't the worst of it. My wagon train is late. Wheel bearings shriek on my lead wagon, and Gen. Thomas will not be pleased to be delayed at the River Line.

As expected, the fighting and skirmishing, and the delay at Roswell Mill, gave the enemy time to cross the Chattahoochee, abandoning most of his formidable "shoupades."

Johnston's chief engineer, Francis Shoup, an Indianapolis lawyer turned Confederate, designed those earthworks and palisades, spaced with pointed projections inspired by the corners of the Spanish fort at St. Augustine.

Sherman remarks on how intelligently the shoupades are built, and plans to go around them.

Gen. Thomas is positioned at the River Line. Yanks spread along thirty miles of river. Schofield to our left, McPherson to our right, keeping the enemy guessing where we'll cross now that the ferryboats are gone. Pontoon units drift, wagon and railroad bridges lie wrecked. Thomas waits for my supply train.

The squeal of wheels won't be ignored. Before leaving

Marietta, I checked everything. I made sure the wagoners did, too.

In the shadows, a figure moves slowly and familiarly. Trouble. I play it easily.

"Out for a morning walk, Private Castleberry?"

His eyes jump. "Just lookin' over your wagons. You all set for today's adventure?"

"The usual."

"Thought I'd offer help."

"Supply line's set."

"Ain't none of my business," he says, and slinks off.

Snooping again. And that phrase "ain't none of my business." What does business mean?

I had checked the grease bucket—enough lubricant for the journey. A wagoner's duty. Yet now, rolling hard, the bearings sing. Too soon. I call a halt and go to the rear axle.

An empty grease bucket dangles there.

Someone's been at my wagon. Castleberry.

Without grease, friction eats wood through the bearings; the heat melts the brass linings and fuses the hub to the axle.

The wheel locks.

I ask down the line. Two wagoners spare extra grease. We lubricate the bearings. Will it hold? By the time we move again, we're an hour late.

The wheels fall silent. Good. The heat and dust don't help. The wagon groans. Did that snake do more? Sweat stings my eyes.

The sun climbs. Delay means hunger, maybe worse. Did the enemy dig in—or cross? Will we run short of ammunition because my ordnance wagon lagged? Will men die? Gen. Thomas will be anxious—furious.

Before the River Line, the baked clay makes hoofbeats sound like hardtack. My nerves go flat with frustration.

Gen. Thomas receives the train. Hearing my account—and the implication of sabotage—he stiffens.

"We'll look into this, Lieutenant. And the other trains will share lubrication."

Relief settles when he confirms the 78th's ordnance wagon is intact. Upriver, Schofield repairs the wagon bridge. Downriver at Paces Ferry, Gen. Howard runs decoy movements. The heat is brutal.

Four days on the River Line are filled with volleys and skirmishes while plans are weighed. Today, Gen. Thomas gives special orders to Col. James Brownlow (1st Tennessee Cavalry), the hero of Lost Mountain.

Known for inventive tactics, he's to clear the rebel rifle pits across the river by any means.

Brownlow surveys Powers' Ferry. The boat's gone. There are two rickety canoes left. He orders steady fire, then takes nine men a mile upstream. They build a makeshift raft, load guns, and cartridge boxes. With musket fire echoing, they strip and swim naked to the far bank. Pale bodies glint as belts go back on. Brownlow leads them naked through the woods.

They charge, yelling and firing. The rebels scatter. Twelve captured, forced to swim back, disarmed. Brownlow returns for more—men strip and swim again, some clinging to horses, Brownlow hauling stragglers across. Forty-eight more prisoners were made to swim into custody. Laughter and pride ripple through the troops.

The next day, banter drifts across the water.

"Hello, Yank!"

"What do you want, Johnny?"

"Can't talk no more."

"How's that?"

"Orders to dry up."

"What for?"

"Jim Brownlow and them Tennessee Yanks swam over naked, took our pits, captured a mess of boys, and made 'em swim back. We got to keep you'uns on your side now."

"Don't count on it. Brownlow's got more tricks up his sleeve when he's wearing one."

"Ha-ha!"

As dusk warms, the bands answer each other. "Dixie." Then "John Brown's Body." "Bonnie Blue Flag." "The Battle Cry of Freedom."

A pause. From the hush, a lone clarinet plays "Home Sweet Home." Silence stretches. Marsh lilies stand witness. Billy Yank and Johnny Reb think of home.

Home. Where I once warned my brother against soldiering. We've grown used to arson and killing. Sometimes I wonder if every Georgia creek must run red before this ends—and whether the weapons we wield are scraping away what makes us human.

Chapter Thirty-One

"He goes, and he goes NOW!" CSA President Jefferson Davis's thunder is heard far and wide across battle lines. He is so infuriated with Joseph Johnston's failure to stop the Union's advance that he is immediately sending into action Gen. John Bell Hood to replace him.

"Hood!" The shock reverberates through the camp. He's known as a battle-hardened commander always ready for a fight. Sherman remembers Hood from their days at West Point. He tells us to watch out. He knows Hood as a flamboyant risk-taker. Nevertheless, Sherman is confident that the risk-taker will lack caution, and he sends a telegram to Ulysses S. Grant.

"Let us give these southern fellows all the fighting they want, and when they are tired, we can tell them we are just warming to the work." William Tecumseh Sherman

At this stage of the Atlanta campaign, we've torn up all but one railroad feeding the city. McPherson moves on Decatur to cut the last line. Schofield presses from the northeast. Our Army of the Cumberland under Gen. Thomas prepares to drive straight across Peach Tree Creek, another soaking march in brutal heat.

The men are keyed up. John Bell Hood, the winner-take-all First Sortie commander charged with our annihilation, is the sort of challenge that stokes a man's blood.

As we march toward what we expect to be the fight at this last natural barrier, a rider pounds in through the rain with a mailbag.

Mail call tightens every throat. What did that bag carry, wine or grief? It smells of damp wool.

George gets a letter, postmarked Marietta, Georgia. Those of us who know him trade glances. He tears it open. His face gives nothing away, only a slow tightening at the mouth. His fingers shake as he folds it back and slips it into his tunic like a charm.

For a moment, I think about how much weight a single sheet of paper can carry, how small victories feel beside someone else's guilt or grief.

At least it isn't from home. Who writes George from Marietta?

The thought snaps away as we refocus. Hood knows Sherman has us advancing in three armies, and he's chosen ours to smash first. It makes sense. Crossing Peach Tree Creek takes time; Hood thinks we'll be sitting ducks.

One o'clock, July 20. We're planted on a ridge, watching Hood marshal his attack. Cheatham east, Stewart west, Hardee center, facing us. Sherman scans with field glasses, calling what he sees to the commanders.

Then—what in God's name? Cheatham starts sliding half a mile farther east. Hardee shifts to keep contact. Stewart follows, closing east by another half mile. I can't help gauging the ground for wagon wheels, even as disbelief creeps in.

Unbelievable. Cheatham shifts again—another half mile.

The dominoes keep falling for three agonizing hours. Hood's theatrics are almost comical. Let him think we're stalled at the creek. We've crossed—and now we're digging earthworks on the far side.

When Hardee finally strikes, Thomas's army meets him head-on. There's no time to load and fire. Close work.

"Fix bayonets! Copy; fix bayonets!" rips down the line.

We drop more of them than they do of us. Bodies splash into the creek. Men wrestle and tumble together in the water. For a heartbeat I hear my son's laughter as he pulls a fish from the lake, then blood spatters my mouth with its iron taste.

A burly mammoth of a rebel rushes at me with blazing fire in his eyes. I know he will soon be on me. I read his face with its shrunken stump where a right ear used to be. But his enormous form and his limp are enough to tell me who he is. Cyrus Braddox is hell-bent on breaking my neck with his bare hands for revenge since Shiloh.

He swings. I duck. The blow clips my head, knocks my hat into the creek. With his rifle arm locking my neck, his free-hand fingers seize my throat. I drop my weight, lower the bayonet, and drive it in.

My hand shakes as I pull the blade free. He folds into the creek, scarlet ribbons spreading in the ripples. The fire leaves his eyes. He tries one last shot—the ball smashes into a tree.

I stand there with blood on my hands. The roar thins to a ring in my ears. I stare into the water, searching for the man I used to be. My fingers tremble—not from cold, but from what they've learned to do.

My glance shifts. Are Archie Clement's bushwhackers here with Big Cyrus? I don't see them. That doesn't mean they aren't close.

When the dust settles, Hood has pulled his whole force

back into Atlanta. In three hours along the wooded ridges and ravines of Peach Tree Creek, we've beaten back his First Sortie.

I've killed before, but with musket fire, not cold steel. My right hand sweats. Knowing how it held the blade is almost too much.

There is an unspoken rule, North and South: bayonets are a last resort.

Was this mine?

Chapter Thirty-Two

I can't believe my eyes. "Ted, who's that kid riding beside Gen. Sherman?" A boy in Yankee blue, rifle in hand, endearing and unsettling all at once. Pets are one thing, and forbidden by code. But children?

"Sherman brought him down from Chattanooga," says Szewzyski. "Johnny Clem. Ran away at nine. He tried to enlist three times before they took him as a drummer boy at eleven. Made his name at Chattanooga by shooting a Confederate officer who demanded his surrender."

I'm stunned but pleased to see Johnny Clem befriend Edmond. Clem shows him how to saw a rifle stock to fit his shoulder, and before long, they're riding patrol wherever we go.

At the same time, my mind won't let go of the French mill women, their flight from terror in Mexico into near servitude at Roswell King's mill, only to be uprooted again by us. I respect their resilience. This war outpaces fiction.

That evening, George asks me to sit with him somewhere quiet. Apprehension tightens.

What now?

He pulls out the Marietta letter we'd all wondered about.

"Gotta tell you something, Will."

I read his face. "We've kept secrets, haven't we?"

"Remember Roswell Mill, when you didn't see me for a few days?"

"I worried about your leg."

"Not my leg. My conscience. I volunteered to process the French women at the Institute. Some soldiers abused them."

"I've heard. It betrays our purpose."

He swallows. "There's a girl, Lydia."

"The one who reached for you?"

"Her. Seventeen. She came to me again, hands out, eyes tight with fear. She was terrified."

He pauses. I wait.

"She threw her arms around me and begged me to protect her. Boxcars were being loaded, the same cars they'd be shipped in. I told myself I was breaking code. We crawled behind cotton bales to talk, away from eyes."

"You hoisted her up."

"I did. Lifted her into the boxcar. Climbed in after."

My worry deepens. "Did she speak English?"

"Enough. She clung to me. I wanted to help her, like you helped Frances. I was drawn to her. Emotions ran high, and she slipped into French."

"I hear you, George. I know you."

He wrestles with it, then continues. "She said something I can't forget, *'Tu me donnes envie du baise.'*"

"Meaning?"

"One woman later told me, 'You make me want to have sex.' Plain talk."

"And?"

"And by then, passion broke the barriers. I know it sounds foolish, consorting with the enemy, but we love each other. She promised to keep in touch. She wrote me."

"The army calls her a traitor," I say. "What does she think?"

"Her letter says it best."

Marietta, Georgia
July 6, 1864

Mon cher Private Hall, sir,

My heart is with you for the protection and love you showed me. I was a textile worker in Normandy when the cotton famine came in 1863. I was sixteen. Mills closed. No rent, no food.

I went to Mexico during the French intervention. A merchant carried us there. In Guadalupe, we found work, but President Juárez drove out the French governor Maximilian. The French people were attacked. We fled, bribed a coffee ship captain to Mobile, and walked to Georgia. Roswell Mill gave us food and shelter for labor.

France is neutral, but Napoleon III wants to favor the Confederacy. The North wants no French empire. Soldiers came. They call us traitors.

We are not traitors. We belong to no side. We are women caught in terror. They will send me to Indianapolis. If I find work, I will wait. If letters are stopped, I will find a way to telegraph. You are my man. I am your woman. I will wait always.

Lovingly,
Lydia Boisvert

He wipes his eye. The camp falls away. I see my friend, not the unsure boy, but a man discovering devotion where zeal, love, and duty knot tight.

"George, Private Hall, sir," I say at last, "I can not fault you. But you could face trial, even execution, for this."

"We risk death daily," he says. "A man follows his conscience. This was real. She wouldn't have asked unless she needed me."

"What do you want from me?"

"We made a pact at Kennesaw. If one of us dies, the other carries words to those we love. Lydia is one of mine."

"I'll honor it," I say. "I'll get word to Lydia, and to your family."

We sleep well.

At dawn, hawks wheel and cry as if summoning us. Hood is bottled in Atlanta now, no retreat left. I wonder how an eleven-year-old drummer boy, romping with Edmond, fits into Sherman's design, and where we fit. Exhilarating. Terrifying.

Recon reports two concentric rings around Atlanta: the inner bristling with guns; the outer trenched, sharpened logs thrust outward. Sentries hold a bare rise east of the city, Bald Hill. An abandoned logger's house sits alone within range. Beyond, Joseph Wheeler's cavalry backs Patrick Cleburne's division.

Sherman works like an orchestra conductor. First, Schofield is sent to wreck the Georgia Railroad toward Augusta. McPherson strikes near the Decatur junction. Troops seize Decatur, posting a field hospital and supply wagons by the courthouse.

Across from it stands the Benjamin Swanton House, ideal for Army of the Tennessee operations. August Hurt's house becomes Sherman's headquarters. Abandoned houses along the Marietta march still haunt me.

Our 78th, with Gen. Leggett under George Thomas, is set on Bald Hill. Why let Cleburne command that view of Atlanta?

I'm glad to serve under Thomas, disowned by his Virginia kin for staying Union, seeking no glory.

As the sun crests, Frank Blair and Manning Force go in hard against Cleburne. Muskets thunder. A shell rips through a trench team, another blows a man apart, a leg, then an arm; his cartridge box lodges in a tree. Smoke and blood thicken the heat.

After four hours, Cleburne withdraws. Union guns crown the hill, Force's doing. Force himself is shot through the face by a minie ball and survives. There's something indomitable about him.

His men reverse the trenches, carving a path toward the city where the enemy faced outward. No time to widen them.

The sun beats down. Jackets open, chests slick with sweat, and we're now in range of Atlanta. Our division hammers the outer works.

Before dawn on July 22, a girl runs to our wagons, breathless. Her father, a miller, is being pistol-whipped by a Confederate general to guide them to our train.

"There's a helper with him," she gasps, "telling him not to shoot the guide. Our mill's a mile south. My father, Case Turner, is leading them the long way. I took the shortcut. I'm Annette Turner. I'm twelve."

Her courage is astonishing. Gen. William H. T. "Shot Pouch" Walker was ordered to hit our rear. Instead, the miller's detour swings Walker north, straight into Grenville Dodge's 16th Corps.

Whether Annette acted from Union loyalty or sheer defiance to save her father, I don't know. Either way, she wagered her life.

In this war, innocence pays dearly.

Chapter Thirty-Three

Shot Pouch Walker doesn't even pause to gather his cavalry. He's bent on smashing my wagon train, and he drives straight into Sweeney's sixteen-shot repeating rifles under Dodge's command. The fighting turns thick. Men drop on both sides, crying out.

Walker spurs into the center, saber flashing, yelling, "Follow me!" He lifts his hat on the saber's tip.

He slashes nothing but air. A Yankee sniper's bullet finds his horse as it rears—then the animal crashes to the rocky ground. Walker staggers up, panting. A sharpshooter's lead punches into his chest. Pathetically few of his men make it out before they, too, lie prone, their mounts wandering off.

Leggett still holds Bald Hill well. He tells us the enemy advance out of Atlanta—meant to start at dawn under Hardee—was delayed five hours. They blame heat, exhaustion, anything. We get sport out of imagining whether our old Lakota friend Pasquale is up to the kind of tricks he pulled at Jackson.

While we speculate, Jose Fleisher comes galloping in from

Sherman's headquarters at Decatur. The horse snorts and strains; Jose looks the same. He folds over his saddle, gasping.

"Cump Sherman…wants me to…tell you, one of our soldiers…in the hospital tent…from the Shot Pouch Walker fight…took a shot, fractured his thigh. They started to prep the leg for amputation. When they pulled his shoe, a paper fell out, the Confederate Secret Service Bureau. The man's a damned rebel spy!"

"You got the name?" I ask.

"Hiram Castleberry," Jose says. "He was what we suspected. Former wagoner knew exactly how to get at you. He played the harmless prankster, so nobody'd peg him as a spy."

"You say he was…?"

"The JAG Corps didn't waste time. The paper said enough. They took him to a firing squad on the Decatur green." Jose's breath comes hard. "When the shots rang out, justice was served."

"It's sickening," I say, "knowing we'll never learn all the damage he did, to our cause and to our men."

"I'll never forget," George says, "seeing him try to poison your horses."

An artillery boom shatters the air. We look up as the lines form like a huge letter L, our forces on the inside of the angle. The short leg is held by Sweeney and Dodge, and my supply wagons stretch along it, feeding Leggett and Thomas on Bald Hill, and Blair below.

Beyond, the ruined Georgia Railroad cuts through the formation, credit to Schofield for tearing it up clean. Farthest from us at the other end sit Morgan Smith and John Logan.

With Hood loose and hungry, I feel steadier knowing Logan anchors that end. He's the kind of soldier who'll hold a lost man from another division in his arms, have an aide pour brandy into his mouth, then stay with him until the man finds his regiment.

In the middle of that thought, new trouble flares below Bald Hill. Wheeler comes dashing back from Decatur to reinforce Hardee's assault at the base of the hill. There, he meets Blair and Sweeney. Thirty minutes of Union musket fire drives them back into the woods. If Hardee had arrived thirty minutes earlier, we might not have been ready.

A gap opens below the hill between Leggett and Blair. Around one o'clock, Cleburne's division pours out of the trees with their rebel yell, only to slam into Sweeney. Texans under Cheatham use the gap to strike Blair's corps.

Then Cleburne comes again, the rebel yell's a blood-curdling scream, half wolf howl, half Apache war cry. We hold until they're twenty yards out, then cut them down. Three times the assaults come, three times the volleys answer. Then we surge from our rough fort and meet them in grim hand-to-hand, fists, clubbed muskets, wrestling, honed steel.

A determined butternut lunges for our banner in Russ Bethel's hands. Russ holds, even as the man wounds him in both legs. Two color guards fall dead, but Russ, bloodied and shaking, whips one rebel in the jugular. The brute staggers, groaning like an animal, and McBurney of Company H slashes him open with a sword. Another rebel strikes Russ's shoulder, knocking him off balance, then one of ours rises and cracks that attacker with a rifle butt. We hold the hill.

The fight grinds on with brutal losses. Nine Confederate regiments press toward Blair's rear. Our artillery throws one-mile guns into the Texans. The 64th Illinois charges, and out of 360 men, only 90 return. Bitter sacrifice. The price of facing John Bell Hood.

In the early afternoon, Gen. James McPherson rides out on

reconnaissance with his orderly and Col. Robert Scott, down a wooded ravine trail.

His horse comes back without him.

Worry spreads, then word from the field hospital: Private George Reynolds, 15th Iowa, found McPherson barely alive and carried him, his arm broken and all, to Surgeon William Gordon. Too late. He was thirty-six. Sherman wept openly.

Grief hits every division. Any one of us would have traded his life to save him. The army feels smaller without James Birdseye McPherson.

Details trickle in. McPherson's party ran into Capt. Frank Beard, 5th Texas, and a corporal. Beard demanded surrender, sword raised. McPherson feigned a salute, wheeled, and bolted. He was shot in the back, the ball cutting through the strap of his field glasses and into his lungs, the surgeon said. Scott, in haste, smashed into a tree. He and the orderly were taken. Scott's broken watch was found, stopped at 2:02 p.m.

The loss is catastrophic. Sherman said the death of the entire Confederate force couldn't balance McPherson's. He replaced him with Illinois' own John "Black Jack" Logan.

The reconnaissance never finished. Cleburne charges again through the gap between Blair and Dodge. Logan orders Dodge right, Blair left, with Col. Martin and three artillery batteries in support. Cleburne withdraws. The heat stays beastly; the whole situation stays tenuous.

Blair worries about Leggett on the hill and sends word asking if he can hold. Leggett answers, "Tell Gen. Blair the hill is as safe as if there wasn't a rebel within a thousand miles."

Another slice of Cleburne's men appears at the edge of a cornfield, advancing on Bald Hill. A Baptist minister, they say, leads them. Blessed are the peacemakers. We volley from our ragtag fort.

Men from Iowa's 4th Division join us until we're ten deep.

We're ordered to fire in rotating lines, front rank shoots, drops; next rank fires under, "Down in front!" and, "Rear men, mind your aim!" The rhythm works.

Then a small figure breaks into view, running across the ground the rebels just crossed. Johnny Clem. Sawed-off musket in hand, dragging a hundred-pound cartridge box stolen straight from the rebel position. Edmond is right behind him, rifle on his shoulder, hauling a second box. Shells whip the air around them.

"Johnny! Edmond!" I shout. "Over here!"

I haul them up into my lead wagon with the ammunition and shove them down into cover. When they can, they're to hop to the next wagon, and the next, until they're out of the line.

I have to trust they'll do it. God, we need that ammo.

On the hill, rebels crawl from trench to trench, using our own digging for cover. Rage rises hot. The bugle sounds again: "Fix bayonets!" We go in, clubbed muskets and cold steel.

In the middle of it, a roar erupts on our right flank. A rebel column slipped through smoke and cannon thunder, through the railroad cut, and formed in our rear. Logan hears his old division is under attack and rides the right flank, black hair streaming, hat waving, shouting, "McPherson and revenge, boys!"

His men answer, "Black Jack! Black Jack!" The combined force retakes the ground and even recovers the batteries abandoned in the assault.

"You all right, George?"

"My calf still aches from Kennesaw," he says, "but I'm okay. You?"

"Good to make it this far," I say.

Chapter Thirty-Four

"One man!" Mortimer Leggett is shouting. The intensity surpasses any battle I've known. My nerves are stretched like rubber bands ready to snap. "Not on one man!" His order is clear: Bald Hill will not be yielded as long as one man remains to pull a trigger.

Ammunition is running dangerously low. Infantrymen, whose cartridge boxes hold a forty-round issue, are scavenging rounds from the dead and wounded scattered across the slope. Men kneel at the edge of Bald Hill, turning bodies with shaking hands, praying the next cartridge will let them reload.

The ordnance wagon started the battle with 100 wooden boxes. Now only two remain. Thank God, Edmond and Johnny hauled two more from behind enemy lines.

At the crest of the hill, officers with swords fight shoulder to shoulder with soldiers wielding bayonets, and many with bare knuckles, while a September breeze snaps battle flags and blades shred regimental banners. Hands slip, slick with blood. Even if you find a cartridge, it's hard to load. The death grapple that ignited around five o'clock has raged for more than half an hour.

They say the wagon train is the lifeblood of the infantry. I've parked the ordnance wagon right at the hill's edge for access, a gamble every wagoner faces, and one I take with dread. As cartridges dwindle, Ketchum grenades see more use. With them comes multiplied danger. We're fighting, as Leggett demands, to the last man if need be. The hand-to-hand fury to hold Bald Hill feels as though it will consume us all.

Then a rebel grenade detonates behind my ordnance wagon, igniting the canvas sun-cover. The breeze, so welcome moments earlier, fans the flames forward toward the cradle of our last two wooden boxes, each packed with a thousand cartridges. No wagoner's nightmare could be worse.

At the crack of the grenade, my lead pair of horses lurches on the uneven slope. I have seconds, seconds to unhitch them before they bolt into the fight, dragging a burning wagon.

With my assistant wagoner Kleist, I rush the trace chains and start unhooking. The metal is scorching. As we fumble at the breast straps, I glance toward the fight and see George Hall taking charge, running downhill toward me, his leg still bandaged. Smoke billows around us. Cannon fire shakes the hill like an earthquake. The noise is numbing.

200 pounds of ammunition still must come off. I thrust the reins into Kleist's hands and send him leading the horses away. I scramble onto the loosened hitch. A quick look inside the wagon tells me Johnny Clem and Edmond have already moved to safer wagons down the line. Burning canvas stings my eyes and lungs.

My gaze snaps back to the cartridge boxes.

A voice cuts through the smoke. Out of nowhere, a hobbling figure, a crutch, Pasquale. He heaves up the first wooden box and passes it to me. I shove it to George and shout, "Run!"

Pasquale lifts the last box and turns to hand it over. The heated wind lashes my face. Flames lick first at cloth, then flesh, arms, and hands. The cartridge box ignites in a blinding fireball.

Pasquale and I are swallowed by the inferno.

A Misty Night--September 22, 1914

Dizziness.

Agonizing numbness.

What...happened?

It is night. Too dark to see clearly, the grass, hills, and forest loom with a sense of danger. Yet, in some strange way, the place feels powerful...hopeful.

I know this place.

This is where I collapsed over the front of a wagon. It is barely recognizable now, as though it burned to cinders long ago and decayed into memory.

Something, something beyond life, has told me to remember.

And I did.

Everything came back. My earliest desire to enlist. My entire soldier's road. My whole army life.

A light appears, brilliant but narrow, as though shining through a tear in a cloak of darkness. It beckons me forward.

I take one step and stop.

I do not want to go. Not yet. I must make sense of what I've remembered. It's all blurred, overwhelming.

Slowly, I turn.

The haze thins. A pair of eyes emerges, pleading eyes. A hand lifts, beckons, then brushes back a lock of auburn hair.

Only then do I understand who stands before me.

Only then do I recognize her voice.

Chapter Thirty-Five

"William, I promised you in the note that I would meet you at the threshold of eternity. I came to help you sort out your difficulty."

I cannot move. Yet her eyes, and that lock of hair, are so convincing. "Louise? Is that you?" The mist swirling around me must be casting bedeviling shadows. "Tell me, tell me, if you can, something I can know. Something to assure me it is you. If it's really you, I need to hold you."

"Chilli Will. Do not embrace me. I have carried through so many years since you died--fifty years to this day. Now that you have retraced everything, the chief thing you must do is to hold on to what you've recollected. Take a moment to untangle the knot, to find a thread of truth through that jumble of emotions troubling you."

"Oh, Louise, I desperately hope that will make sense of my fragmented loyalties. But I need something first. Please, fill me in on what happened after the blast that turned my body into cinders. That's the part of the equation I yearn to know. Did we win the war?"

"We did, William. But with many more casualties. There was a wild celebration in Zanesville, and all over. So much time has passed since those lovely days and nights of your furlough. You died before you could be notified that I had birthed you a beautiful daughter. Abigail is grown and married now, named for the biblical peacemaker."

My son Johnny...is he well?"

"Johnny graduated near the top of his class in Zanesville, then from the Peabody Conservatory of Music, studying drama. He has played at the Metropolitan Opera Company."

"That's beyond gratifying, Louise, a lot beyond Friar Tuck! And George Hall, did he survive the war?"

"He did. He recovered, joined Sherman's March to the Sea, fulfilled his reenlistment, and came to visit me. He told me how you fought and died at Bald Hill. He also went to Jacob Glessner's estate and presented your sister Margaret with the treasures from your tent, the CSA belt buckle, the boatman's luggage tag, the *Courier* clipping I gave you, and that silly little card from church, all clipped to one verse. She placed them with your Vicksburg splinter."

"Fulfilling our death pact sealed at Kennesaw. Did George tell you about his lady friend?"

"Did he! Oh, William, thank you for helping George at Roswell. Lydia waited for him at Union Station in Indianapolis, just as she promised. He brought her to Zanesville. They have been happily married for many years."

"Louise, that lady has more stamina than I knew. I'm so glad for them."

"Guess who was George's best man."

"Sam? Alexander?"

"Edmond. Johnny Clem made the army his career, and if they could find Johnny, they could find Edmond. They were heroes together."

"Heroes?"

"After Atlanta surrendered, those two boys were on patrol and came upon a Confederate home flying a white flag. The owner begged for mercy; his nineteen-year-old daughter, Nancy, was in labor. Johnny sent Edmond to Gen. Thomas while he guarded the house. Thomas spared it and sent a Union surgeon. The baby, Anna Holt, lived to tell the story."

"Heroes indeed. How about your brother Alex?"

"Wounded at Stones River, but he pressed on and served through Bentonville. He farms outside Massillon now."

"I can hardly believe how much time has passed."

"So much time, my dear Chilli Will."

"And you? How was your life?"

"I lived fully and died of natural causes, surrounded by those I loved—except you. When I entered the spirit world, I searched for you. Then I remembered the note I slipped into your pocket at the station, that I would meet you at the threshold of eternity—and I hurried here. Forgive me for making you wait."

"I wasn't waiting. I was too foggy to remember your promise. The foibles of being human. But you've cleared the way. I feel the knot loosening."

She lifts her chin, inhales, then exhales strongly. "Beautiful."

"I couldn't release the trauma of not being home at Mary's death. Yet I believed I had to stay and help unite a divided country. I saw women strained and abused throughout the war. I didn't know it then, but their trials echoed Mary's unfair passing. And still, most of them bore resilience and survived.

"There were quarrels among officers, competing when they should have cooperated. Schofield's old jealousy of Thomas lingered, juvenile animosities, long lived."

"You lived through many turns in your tours of duty."

"I see it now as growth rings on a tree, good growth and poor. We begin with gentleness, often given by a woman. Then competition intrudes. It can degrade the soul. But when we carry forward that first kindness, reciprocate respect, life becomes a jewel."

"William, you've made peace with the quandary that troubled you."

"Louise, your love helped me do it. I'm ready to walk into the light. Take my arm. Are you ready to enter with me?"

"Marching on."

Acknowledgments

I am indeed indebted to William Tyre of Glessner House and his staff in Chicago; to Laura Varner of the Gen. John A. Logan Museum in Murphysville, IL; to Former Home of Gen. George H. Thomas, Washington, D. C.; to Doug Hansen of the Hansen Wheel and Wagon Shop of Letcher, SD; to John J. Glessner's *Story Of a House*, to Thomas N. Stevenson's *1865 Account of the 78th Ohio Infantry*; to David Lowenherz, ed., *Letters From America's Wars*; to Robert Redd's *St. Augustine and the Civil War*; to the *Ohio History Collection*; to *The National Tribune*; to the online forum *Civil War Talk*; along with myriad journals and online sources; to the Flagler College Womn's Volleyball team; to my writing coach Killian Wolf; to Legacy Collections Publishing; to my colleague Prof. Jean Gould; to my sister Carol Haeussner; to my daughter Prof. Keira McCoy Hicks; and to my loving wife, the late Prof. Sandra Remieres Glessner, for her patience. She loved playing "Soupy, Soupy, Soupy" on her bugle!

Richard H. Glessner
January 5, 2026

About the Author

Richard Glessner, at 92, is a retired psychology professor and college chaplain. Born to American parents in Iraq and schooled in Beirut, Lebanon, his international interest led to adopting four international children with his wife, Sandy, now deceased. Educated at the University of Chicago, he has authored four books, but Marching On is his first novel, based on the military service of a distant Ohio relative. Currently, he is working on another Civil War novel involving the divided North vs South loyalties of two sisters in his family tree. He has worked on archaeological digs and as a lighthouse docent. Living in St. Augustine, Florida, he and his soulmate Bonnie love to support the Flagler College Women's Volleyball Team, of which he is their honorary grandfather.

www.ingramcontent.com/pod-product-compliance
Lightning Source LLC
Chambersburg PA
CBHW031040160726
47991CB00005B/1962

9 798995 157205